AWARDS FOR JULIE BURTINSHAW'S NOVELS

The Freedom of Jenny
NOMINATED: Stellar Award

Adrift
SELECTED: Canadian Children's Book Centre "Our Choice" List
SHORTLISTED: Manitoba Young Readers' Choice Award
NOMINATED: Canadian Library Association Book of the Year
Chocolate Lily Book Award
Red Cedar Award

Dead Reckoning
SELECTED: Canadian Children's Book Centre "Our Choice" List
NOMINATED: Chocolate Lily Award
Diamond Willow Award
Red Cedar Award

THE PERFEC

CUT

RAINCOAST BOOKS
Vancouver

Raincoast Books gratefully acknowledges the financial support of the Province of British
Columbia through the BC Arts Council and the Book Publishing Tax Credit and
the Government of Canada through the Canada Council for the Arts and the Book
Publishing Industry Development Program (BPIDP).

Editorial contributions by Tonya Martin and Joanna Karaplis
Cover and interior design and illustrations by Five Seventeen / picapica.ca
Author photo © James Moffat

Lyrics are from Nomeansno's "Dad" (p. 11), "Small Parts Isolated and Destroyed" (p. 28),
"Disappear" (p. 160, 172, 214, 233), "Revenge" (p. 238), and "State of Grace" (p. 257).
Courtesy of Nomeansno.

Library and Archives Canada Cataloguing in Publication

Burtinshaw, Julie, 1958–
    The perfect cut / Julie Burtinshaw.

ISBN 13: 978-1-55192-816-6
ISBN 10: 1-55192-816-7

    I. Title.
PS8553.U69623P47 2008   jC813'.6   C2007-904845-5

Library of Congress Control Number: 2007933942

Raincoast Books
9050 Shaughnessy Street
Vancouver, British Columbia
Canada v6p 6e5
www.raincoast.com

In the United States:
Publishers Group West
1700 Fourth Street
Berkeley, California
94710

Printed in Canada by Webcom

    09 10 11 • 5 4 3 2

THE
PERFECT
CUT

Julie Burtinshaw

For trusting me with your stories, for sharing your experiences—I thank you

Acknowledgements

This book would not have been possible without the help and encouragement of many people, but I'd like to give particular thanks to:

My fabulous and talented editor Tonya Martin for her insight, her support and her excellent sense of humour.

To Jesse Finkelstein, Associate Publisher, Raincoast Books, for believing in this project from the start.

To Joanna Karaplis, Editorial/Publishing Assistant, Raincoast Books, for her painstaking attention to detail and calming influence.

Special thanks to Rod McFarland, who planted and watered the seeds out of which this book was born.

Sincere gratitude to Tom Holliston, NoMeansNo, for taking the time to read this story while still in development.

Thanks to Karen Schauber for her advice and feedback on therapist/patient interactions, as well as her insight into counselling teenagers and families.

And of course, gratitude and thanks to my family for their ongoing love and support while accompanying me through the long process of writing yet another novel.

A suicidal person seeks to end all feelings. I cut to feel better.

"I'm seriously considering leaving home..."
NOMEANSNO, "DAD"

One

In the bathroom I can spend hours watching the steel and the soft skin—imagining the eventual collision between electropositive element and organic matter. I never cut.

I never tell the truth.

I lie.

Two

Finding a razor blade that would do the job hadn't been the easiest thing in the world. His mom's Venus didn't cut it, so in the end he went to the hardware store. Not the one near his house because someone might recognize him and ask him questions. It amused him to pretend that people were interested in him. So instead of walking up the street to the hardware store, he took the bus downtown, where nobody knows anybody. He bought a pack of single-edged razors, the old-fashioned kind that he imagined his grandfather might have used to shave. He was prepared to tell the clerk that he needed them to scrape stickers off his car window. The clerk didn't ask. The clerk didn't care.

Nobody does.

Three

Bryan stood motionless in the centre of his room; in his hand he gripped the old-fashioned razor blade he'd bought earlier that day. Out of the corner of his eye, he saw that his bedside clock read 5:16 p.m. He didn't have a lot of time until the parents came home, but he had enough time if he got going soon. He didn't like to rush into it, because he loved this part; saw it as the physical equivalent of a great hook, like the opening riff in "In-A-Gadda-Da-Vida."

Finally, he lifted his T-shirt and pressed the flat edge of the razor against soft skin. Cold comfort. The tight ball of anticipation that had been festering in his gut all day began to uncoil like a rattlesnake poised to strike. He moved slowly, methodically, and when he could wait no longer, he ran the steel blade with unhurried precision across his taut stomach. He cut shallow, but a little deeper than the last time—just enough to slice a thin red line two centimetres above his belly button. The flesh opened easily, and the blood seeped through pale skin.

Unconsciously, he held his breath, partially to keep his abs tight, partially to wait for the pain to go away. Not the physical pain; the cutting didn't hurt. If only it did. He felt merely a sensation, and with that sensation came relief—a confirmation of existence. If he had to put it into words, he might say, "For a little while, I don't feel empty, or angry or sad. I feel alive, as if I am a real person." He might add, "But never for long enough."

The blood rushed to fill the opening before easing to a trickle and clotting, as he'd known it would. He let out his breath slowly, and something close to a smile played about his lips. He used his T-shirt to swipe his damp eyes so that he could study his handi-work carefully.

A *perfect cut*, Michelle whispered in his ear. He shivered as her cold breath touched his skin. *Just the way I showed you.* He turned toward her, feeling her approval cloak him from the cold like a coat.

But there was no Michelle. What had he expected?

Still, that didn't mean he'd imagined her. Or did it? His eyes travelled through his room, but except for the shadows of the dying day, he found himself completely alone. Only then did he feel the sting of the incision. He drew his curtains open. Outside, the sun bled into the horizon, but there was enough natural light for him to admire the fresh carve. The new cut lay between his belly button and his rib cage. Above the cut, four faint white lines scarred his flesh—a dual set of railway tracks, each one a permanent reminder of his existence. Using a square of white toilet paper, he dabbed the fresh wound. Next, he folded the tissue carefully in half, setting it in the bottom of his sock drawer far from prying eyes. Already, there were others there. Five altogether—five perfect rectangles arranged side by side, each marked by a pale line of blood. He counted them and then counted them again to be sure. Uneven numbers bothered him, meant that he would have to go back to the razor sooner.

His fixation on odd numbers had started just days after Michelle left. He remembered the date in his mind. Over a year ago now: July 7, 2007. Seven. Seven. Seven. Perfect numbers. Numbers to avoid. At first it had just been sevens, but gradually, over the past year, he'd begun to avoid all odd numbers.

It worried him because thinking about stuff like that led to a whole new set of problems and questions. Questions like, "am I different from other people?" He'd always felt like a bit of an outsider. When he was a lot smaller, he'd investigated this situation with disappointing results:

"Mama, how do I know if I'm normal?"

"You are so silly. Of course you're normal, maybe smarter than boys your age, and for sure more handsome."

She'd kissed him on the top of his head and gone back to what she was doing, which had probably been something to do with her garden or the plants that brought colour and scent into the house.

"Daddy, how do I know if I'm normal?"
"What are you talking about? Of course you're normal."

Bryan couldn't remember what his dad had done, but he knew for sure it wouldn't have had anything to do with a kiss on the head—more likely he'd returned to poring over the stock quotes on his computer or oiling the chain on his bike to perfection.

"Michelle, how do I know if I'm normal?"
"If you have to ask, then you're not."

As usual, Michelle hit the nail on the head. "Anyway, in this family, how can anybody be 'normal'?"

She'd leaned over and tickled him and he had adored her because she was so much older and wiser. Michelle always threw stuff like that at him. Michelle never wanted to be normal. She went out of her way not to be like other people—to be different meant to be better, and like everything else she did, she pulled it off with a confidence Bryan longed for.

How long had he been frozen in front of his dresser, his eyes glued on his socks, his mind focused on yesterdays? A minute? An hour? He ran his hand across the smooth, dustless surface as if the answer lay at the tip of his fingers. Like everything else in their house, this piece of furniture reflected his mom's love of beautiful things—the most expensive, the most well-designed, the most elegant—and he slipped back to a time, not so long ago, when she would bounce her decorating ideas off him, when it was he who accompanied her on forays into antique shops and auctions. He had felt her enthusiasm as keenly as he now felt her apathy. Angered at the memory, he slammed the drawer closed; it didn't make a sound, and the silence made him want to cut again.

"Save it for those special moments," Michelle had advised. "Times when you really have no choice." By that time, there were few places on Michelle's body that hadn't felt the knife blade, or the angry burn of a cigarette.

Before:
Bryan and his mom are in the back garden. It's hot. The sun beats down, but it's okay 'cause Mom has made lemonade. It's the real thing, and Bryan loves the smell of fresh lemons. His hands are dirty. They've been gardening, planting vegetable seeds—carrots, lettuce, tomatoes and leeks. "Pretty soon, you'll see the sprouts," Mom tells him.

He's eleven. His mom is pretty, even though streaks of dirt smudge her face and her dark hair is tangled. He knows other moms, but his mom is the best. She knows all about plants. He likes to hear her stories about when she travelled around Europe before she married his dad. She wanted to own her own flower shop, and she took pictures of flower arrangements so she could copy them when she opened her store. Just before she returned to Canada, a thief stole her camera and she lost all her photos. "At first I was really mad, but in the end, it didn't matter because I'd stored all the photos in my head." She laughs because the thief didn't get the best of her, and her eyes sparkle like they do when she sees beauty or justice or just plain fun. Bryan is quiet, thinking about the impossibility of those little seeds turning into vegetables, and how great the lemonade tastes.

The back door swings open. Michelle is silhouetted in the frame. She is tall for her age and could be mistaken for a much older girl. Her stance is defiant. Dad says she has 'attitude.' Bryan wants some of that one day, too.

"Mom," she calls. Mom looks up. Michelle's naturally blonde hair is now black. "What do you think?" She spins around, laughing.

Mom knows that at fifteen, Michelle's hair colour is as unpredictable as her moods. Unlike Dad, Mom knows that argument is futile. "I love it," she replies. "Come on out and join us. I've got a jug of homemade lemonade."

"It's too hot outside."

"Why don't you put on some shorts and a tank top?" In spite of the heat, Michelle wears jeans, 'ripped for air conditioning,' and a long-sleeved shirt.

"I'll just take a glass up to my room." She strides over to where they sit beneath the apple tree and accepts the offered drink. Her nails, like Mom's, are short and there are calluses on the tips of her fingers.

"Thanks." She lands a playful punch on Bryan's shoulder. "When you're done gardening, come on upstairs and I'll teach you a new song."

"I love your hair," says Bryan. "Mom, can I get black hair?" Mom rolls her eyes, pretending frustration, but they both know she doesn't mind.

"Thanks, Little Bro," says Michelle.

She raises her glass to him, turns and saunters off. After she is gone, Mom looks worried. Bryan knows why. Dad won't like the new hair colour. He never does. They all know what he'll say. Something like, "It's a waste of time and money. Why can't you accept the hair you were born with?"

When Michelle goes inside, Bryan and his mom finish their lemonade and go back to planting their vegetable garden. All afternoon they dig in the dirt, and while they dig and cover the seeds with fresh compost mixed in with the dark soil, the sound of Michelle playing guitar drifts out of her bedroom window and serenades them.

"No matter what your dad says about her hair," Mom says, "she is a damn good guitar player." Bryan can tell by her tone that Mom is proud of his big sister and so he is, too.

Michelle eventually puts away her Stratocaster and stands at her bedroom window, sipping her lemonade. It tastes like summer and reminds her of when she was a little girl. Below her, Bryan and Mom create their garden. It is a small plot, but she knows it will yield a large crop. Mom has a green thumb, and Bryan learns quickly. Part of her wishes she could throw on a pair of shorts and a tank, like Mom suggested, and join them planting seeds. But she can't. She is surprised at the wave of nostalgia that washes over her. She misses the days when all three of them did stuff together. She misses being a kid.

She can't wear shorts and T-shirts, skirts or tank tops. Even though she has abstained for a week and there are no fresh carves, the scars are visible. She hopes that one day they will fade. She's determined not to cut herself ever again, but thinking something and doing it are never the same. Still, she is strong and she might succeed.

Bryan's giggling. His delight rises to her bedroom window. He is still a little guy, but that will change. Bryan will be twelve this summer. And next year, he'll go to high school. Soon, Michelle will be sixteen and she'll get her driver's licence. She'll take him driving. Bryan adores her. She can see it in his eyes, and she loves him back, even if he is a bit of a wimp. Michelle feels very protective of Bryan, because Dad can be a real A-hole, and Bryan refuses to stand up for himself.

Michelle wishes it were different. She reflects on how Bryan just looks down when Dad berates him, how he does exactly what he's told, even if he disagrees, how he almost believes that he is as useless as Dad intimates. Michelle says what's on her mind, and she doesn't care if it pisses people off. For some weird reason, Dad gets this, and so he doesn't boss her around or lecture her much. He'd wig out if he knew what she'd done today. She opens the window a little wider, hoping for a breeze to cool off her room so she can play comfortably, and then she plants herself in front of the full-length mirror on the back of her bedroom door and sticks out her tongue. She checks to make sure there is no infection before admiring the silver stud. One of these days, she'll have to tell them. Dad will freak. Bryan will want one, and Mom—well— Mom surprises her sometimes. She might just like it.

Yup, one day she'll have to 'fess up, but not today. She plugs her guitar into her amp and begins to play. Pretty soon, she forgets about everything but the music.

Four

Bryan surfaced in a fog, as if he'd been pulled abruptly from a deep sleep, wondering how he'd ended up standing in the upstairs hallway, metres away from Michelle's bedroom door. He attempted to blink away the grogginess, but his thoughts were unclear, even after several minutes. Not only were the flashbacks, so infrequent in the beginning, becoming more common, the time gaps were increasing, as if the line between the past and the present were dissolving. Would that line one day dissolve completely? He closed his eyes and mentally listed what he knew about the past twelve hours: he'd been at school all day—hadn't skipped a class. He'd taken his time getting home, stopping at the second-hand bookstore where he'd picked up a Sudoku magazine and a tattered copy of *The Doors*. He remembered thumbing through the pages, until he came to a picture of Jim Morrison pounding out a song, oblivious to anything else. Michelle loved The Doors. She'd taught him to play "The End," and they often played it together. At the time, he hadn't been aware of the irony in the lyrics. And now, he found himself standing outside her room, half convinced that if he could see through the solid wood of her door, she'd be in there, head bent over her Stratocaster Rosa Hurricane, her long hair obscuring her profile, and she'd look up at him, and say, "Come on in, Bry. Need some help with math?"

He took a deep breath and moved four paces to her door. Closed. Locked, probably, but he couldn't bring himself to turn the handle.

The Michelle Shrine. Out of bounds for over a year now.

He slowly backed away from her door, the thick Persian carpet muffling the sound of his footsteps. Four steps to the middle of the hall, six to the bathroom and four more to the sink. How many minutes had he been standing there? Five? Fifteen? No way of knowing ... He listened to the sounds of the house, but heard only his own short, rapid breathing. The silence told him the parents were not home, yet.

> *One, two, three, four,*
> *Don't look at the other door.*

He knew one sure way to get back to the present.

After, at the sink, he held the razor under steaming-hot water. He couldn't detect blood. It had been a fast, clean cut, no more than three centimetres long. He dabbed at it with a piece of toilet paper and washed the razor. The hot water did its job. Clean and sterilize. Rinse away the trace amount of blood. Watch the bad go down the drain. He imagined the invisible DNA washing through the pipes, disappearing. He dried the razor and put it in the cabinet, then he washed his hands, counting slowly to sixty to make sure he didn't miss any germs that might be hiding in the cracks of his skin or under his fingernails. Another neat square of toilet paper joined the five others in his sock drawer.

He retraced his steps carefully, returning to his room where he stripped off his shirt and threw it into the laundry basket to join yesterday's jeans, dirty socks and assortment of T-shirts—all black. He didn't like to wear colour, didn't like endorsements. *Not my job to be a walking billboard for Nike or Reebok.*

He considered himself to be the most-principled unprincipled guy he knew.

He grinned, feeling something, instead of just dead. He put on a clean shirt, careful to hold it away from his stomach so as not to irritate the cut. Downstairs, he heard the low hum of conversation. Pots and pans rattled, water ran, cooking smells—onions and garlic—drifted up the stairs, almost masking the smell of chicken.

They were home.

Mostly his dad did the cooking. Bryan and his mom cleaned up after dinner. This had once been the 'kids' job,' when they were plural, but Mom stepped in to help him when he became an only child.

To his surprise, dinner smelled pretty good. Bryan's stomach rumbled. He couldn't remember if he'd eaten all day, but in spite of his hunger, the energy to eat eluded him. Food wasn't the problem, but the thought of their nightly sit-down-and-pretend-everything-is-cool dinner was daunting. It hadn't been bad when Michelle was there to even out the numbers, balance the scales. It was a theory. Truth? He couldn't tell anymore. Maybe he'd made her into a saint like the rest of them had.

He wished his brain would shut up. A CD and a smoke seemed like a good distraction. He pushed PLAY on his CD player and closed his bedroom door before lighting a cigarette. He leaned halfway out the window to smoke it. His dad had a nose like a bloodhound, and Bryan didn't need the lecture right now.

He'd only recently taken up the habit, and the smoke burned his eyes. He closed them against the late-afternoon sun. Fall had always been Michelle's favourite season. "September is the real New Year," she'd told him. "It's the beginning of everything, not January. Think about it, summer ends. We go back to school and into a new grade and everyone gets into a routine. January is half-way through the year—at least that's how it feels to me."

Thinking of her made him smile until he really thought it out, and then it hurt. He opened his eyes and fixed his gaze on the ground below. He imagined falling, but couldn't—a coward in the end. He inhaled deeply and considered that perhaps, by taking up cigarettes, he had simply opted for a slower, more drawn-out suicide. He grinned at the thought and tossed his smoke into the flowerbed before diving onto his bed to surrender himself to the music:

> *There's one thing that I have learned*
> *All God's children will get burned . . .*

Music always helped him to forget. Music replaced the chaos in his head and allowed him some peace. A soft knock on his door shattered his short-lived inner tranquility. "Bryan, dinner's ready." His mom opened the door and peeked in. Her forehead creased when she saw him prone on his bed. "Are you feeling sick?" She walked quickly to him and placed her hand on his forehead.

He was tempted to fake illness, but his stomach won over. "No, Mom. I'm okay. Just taking it easy." He sat up and swung his legs over the side of his bed. "I'll be down in a sec."

"We're having chicken. Your favourite," she added, smiling, as if chicken could save them all.

"Yeah. When I was ten." He shook his head. "I guess I grew up while you were busy freezing time."

"Oh . . . well . . ." She backed slowly out of his room but did not take her eyes off him. She'd never been good at hiding concern or worry. He'd hurt her. He hadn't intended to. He was just being honest.

She reached up and flicked at an invisible hair in front of her eyes. Michelle did the same thing when she felt uncomfortable about anything. Bryan, on the other hand, had other ways to make himself feel better. As soon as Mom left his room, he reached under his bed where he kept a bottle of vodka and downed a quick shot. Liquid courage, so to speak.

He hadn't expected her. Mom rarely ventured upstairs. Dad, never. If they wanted him, they'd either yell up the stairs, or call him on his cell. They weren't lazy, they were scared shitless of the other room, the musty, preserved one that lay at the top of the stairs. He'd come to terms with it because he had no choice. But they chose to pretend it didn't exist.

Even before, the second floor had belonged entirely to the kids. Their bedrooms lacked nothing in space or comfort. Mom had made sure of that. Each kid's room had a top-of-the-line computer, a TV, the latest video-gaming system, and an adjoining bathroom. Pretty deluxe.

Bryan had been in enough of his friends' houses to realize that he had a lot more stuff than most kids his age. No one could ever accuse Dad of not being a hard worker—the guy never stopped. Money made their world turn, yet nobody ever talked about it in their house, just like nobody wore their shoes inside, or drank straight out of the milk jug or left the toilet seat up. Dad made the rules, and they followed them. In exchange, Bryan had all the privacy in the world, and that meant he could pretty much do as he pleased without having to explain himself.

And he had secrets—stuff he'd rather keep to himself. Who didn't? Secrets—even the good ones—set you apart from others. And the bad ones? They ate away at your core. Bryan knew this from experience. In fact, sometimes he imagined his insides being gnawed away by the things he couldn't tell anybody—the dark snippets of information that set him apart from others—from Mom and Dad.

Not that they cared enough to ask. An invisible border divided the house into two countries: the upstairs belonged to Bryan, the downstairs to his parents. Bryan knew there were times when his mother ventured into his territory to visit *The Michelle Shrine* and every couple of days, Stella, their housekeeper, climbed the stairs to the second floor with bucket and mop, broom and dustpan in hand.

Stella had been their nanny, and once upon a time, she'd lived with them in a small room off the playroom in the basement. These days, Bryan rarely saw her—weird, considering she'd once been such a big part of his life. She'd learned not to enter Bryan's room if he was at home, but she existed in his clean, ironed clothes folded into drawers or sweaters hanging neatly in his closet. She existed in the antiseptic smell of his spotless bathroom. The vacuumed carpets and squeaky clean windows screamed Stella, as did his books and CDs stacked in piles that had to be rebuilt because she didn't understand the importance of numbers.

The old Stella, the dark-haired, slender Filipina whom he had adored as a second mother, existed for Bryan somewhere in his jumbled memory. Shadowy memories of her warm hand enfolding his as they walked to and from school. Her soft lips brushing his forehead after bath-and-story time. Her lilting voice assuring him that a mug of honey and lemon, followed by a good night's sleep, would chase away his sore throat and runny nose by morning. Her slim body jumping for joy on the sidelines of the soccer field every single time he scored a goal—or even came close. Her big black eyes, wet with tears, watching him as he said goodbye to Michelle for the last time. It had been Stella who'd wrapped her strong arms around him when his own parents had been too stricken by grief to comfort him. And it had been Stella who had sat up with him that first night when he'd come home from the hospital. He didn't know if he'd pushed her love away or if she'd taken it herself, but the results were the same, and now they barely acknowledged each other's presence.

He thought that maybe he still loved her, but doubted that she could love him back. Her meticulous cleaning would have surely unearthed some of his secrets. After all, if a dust ball could not escape her notice, it was unreasonable to suppose a pack of smokes, or a bottle of vodka, or a flat-edged razor, or tiny squares of folded toilet paper would escape her attention, wasn't it? And even if she hadn't noticed, he'd made it pretty clear that he didn't want her around.

Somewhere in the transition between nanny and housekeeper, between Michelle being at home and Michelle being gone, Bryan stopped looking to Stella for guidance. No longer did he depend on her gentle, yet firm, tone of voice insisting he pick up his clothes, or her encouraging smile to brighten his day, or her soft touch while she was putting a Band-Aid on a scraped knee.

He avoided her when he could, and if he couldn't, he muttered an unintelligible greeting and disappeared into an empty room. He discovered a capacity for unkindness in himself and he honed his newfound skill on her. Yet, if she suspected what went on behind his closed door, she said nothing. If she wished it had been him and not Michelle who disappeared, she never let on.

While Bryan understood Stella's withdrawal, his father did not. "She used to be part of the family; now she creeps around the house like a mouse. Sometimes I think she sneaks up behind me on purpose. If she hadn't been with us for so long, I'd let her go."

"You can't just let people go," Mom retorted, without conviction, because she knew it wasn't true.

"Well, if she doesn't pull up her socks and make an effort, it might come to that. You can't go through life with an attitude like that and expect to be rewarded." He aimed a pointed look at Bryan.

Dad's lectures. What did Michelle call them? Oh yeah. *The Rules of Life.* "Don't know how my world would turn without your input," she'd say to his face, and behind his back she'd roll her eyes and do whatever she wanted. He never heard the sarcasm. Maybe he just didn't want to. After all, he could control almost everything in his life except for Michelle.

And yet, Dad loved her the most.

Bryan entered the kitchen as Dad was putting dinner on the table. Mom, already seated, absently looked up. "Oh, good. You're here and just in time." She handed him the newspaper she'd been reading. "Can you put this on the coffee table for me?"

He did as he was asked, keeping his eyes on the floor. The new slash on his stomach, no longer numb, had really begun to sting. He resisted the urge to touch it, to tear at it. He took his seat at the table instead. "Smells good," he said.

"It'd better be, and 'Hello' to you." His father (who was tall and often mistaken for handsome rather than intimidating) some-how made the greeting sound like an order.

"Hey," Bryan answered.

"Hay? Hay is for horses." The cold eyes cancelled the half smile. "Would have been nice if you'd helped to set the table."

Bryan shrugged. "Sorry." He sat down and began to slide the salt and pepper shakers purposefully across the table, only stopping when they were lined up perpendicular to his plate. Two in a row, like wooden soldiers.

"Let it go, Mike. Let's not get into an argument tonight." Mom helped herself to a small scoop of mashed potatoes. Even a little kid couldn't miss the small vein throbbing at her temple.

Mike, Michel, Michelle. It occurred to Bryan that his sister had been named after their dad. "How'd you guys pick my name?"

Mom looked at him quizzically, but before she could say a word, Dad cut in with, "It was tough. We'd always wanted a Michel, af-ter me, but Michelle seemed close enough, and we didn't expect we'd have a son, so when you came along we named you after a singer we both liked."

"Who?"

"Bryan Adams."

"Bryan Adams?" Bryan sighed. That really sucked. "You mean the guy who sings 'Cuts Like a Knife'?" Irony was alive and well in the Bianchi household. "The guy who Mom listens to all the time?"

"That's the guy," Mom grinned, pleased that he knew the name of her favourite singer.

"So you didn't think about naming me after, say, a grandfather or great-grandfather, or some other ancestor?"

"You were kind of a surprise." Dad laughed. "We'd pretty much completed our family when you came along."

"Yeah, well, that explains a lot," Bryan muttered, dumping half of the contents of the gravy boat over his mashed potatoes.

Dad glared at him across the table. "If you want to be heard, speak up. If you don't want to be heard, shut up." Laugh. They'd heard it before. Only Dad found it funny.

Tell him to go to hell. Michelle slouched against the wall opposite Bryan, arms crossed and looking really pissed off.

"Why don't *you* go to hell," he snapped back at her. She threw her head back and let out a peal of laughter. *Now you're in for it.*

And he should have been, but his mom didn't say a word. His dad didn't say a word. When he mustered the guts to look up from his plate, they were both staring at him, cutlery posed mid-air, mouths open.

See, you've got to bully a bully. Michelle punched at an invisible opponent, dancing on light feet. He ignored her, focused instead on trying to figure out this new dynamic. He ignored his parents, too, acting as if nothing untoward had occurred, as if they weren't both staring at him like they'd seen a ghost. And who knew? Maybe they had. Instead, he picked up his fork and started to eat, still hungry. Mom did the same, and pretty soon even Dad stopped looking so blown away and turned his attention to dinner.

"Please," and "thank you," and "may I have the salt?" and "would you like a little more gravy?" and "this is delicious" interrupted the wailing silence. Sound of knife against fork, of clinking glasses. And all the time, Michelle's chair—empty, yet weighed down by memories.

I miss you, Bry. He turned to where she'd been only minutes ago, but she'd gone. She didn't appear on command. Bryan blinked rapidly, suddenly feeling something when he least expected it. Seeing *her,* hearing *her,* he could handle, but not her empty chair across the table from him. Looking at it made him ache, but he couldn't drag his eyes away.

Big sister Michelle. Michelle who could talk to anyone. Michelle who had Dad all figured out.

"...see if I can catch the news." They'd been talking to each other, and Bryan hadn't really heard a word. Dad stood up. "Make sure you help your mom with the dishes. I did all the cooking." He sounded like a little kid.

When Bryan heard the den door click shut, he turned to his mom and grinned, "That's a relief." Usually she sided with him, saw how Dad hurt him. But this time, she paid him no attention. "Mom? Mom?" he repeated, raising his voice.

"Hmm? Sorry. What?" She chewed her top lip and focused on an invisible spot somewhere on the ceiling.

"Mom, are you okay?"
She sighed. "I'm really not hungry. I pretend hunger, but truthfully I wonder why I bother eating at all."

Bryan looked at her. "Mom? What's up?" Her face crumbled. Tears trickled out of the corners of her eyes—eyes masked by pain. "I'm sorry, Mom."

"Oh, Bryan." She reached over and covered his hand with hers. "That's not what I meant at all. You don't have a thing to apologize for. It's not your fault. None of it."

Bryan jerked his hand away and stood up, knocking his chair over. He hated being touched, and he hated that she made him feel so guilty. He scratched his stomach, and his cut, itchy now, began to bleed.

"Mom, thanks for dinner. I've got stuff to do. Homework and stuff." He righted his chair and began to retreat from the kitchen, pausing when he remembered his dad's order, veiled as a request, to clear the plates from the table.

"Leave it, Bryan. I'll do the dishes if you have homework." She spoke so softly he had to move closer to hear what she said.

"Thanks." He left the kitchen, aware of her dull eyes following him to the foot of the stairs. He counted each footstep carefully, even though he'd memorized the numbers long ago: thirty to the bottom of the stairs, if he took large strides. Another twenty to the top landing. *One, two, three, four, five, six, seven, eight, nine, ten, eleven, twelve, thirteen, fourteen, fifteen, sixteen, seventeen, eighteen, nineteen, twenty.*

Once in his room, Bryan collapsed on his bed. He felt queasy, but preferred that to feeling nothing. The area around his sinuses throbbed. He buried his head under his pillow and wished he could cry, acknowledge the hurt. Not feeling hurt. Feeling hurt. Not feeling anything. Feeling too much. Another screwed-up family meal. Mom in tears. *What a jerk I am. Bad, bad, bad.*

A little later, Bryan stood in front of the bathroom mirror, holding the razor blade to his throat. He had no intention of killing himself, but sometimes he fantasized about it. In a heartbeat, he would take on that person—his mirror image—who gazed back at him, expressionless. He stared at his reflection, and his reflection peered back at him, and he realized how much he hated mirrors. He hated seeing the imperfection called Bryan Bianchi—but tonight he made himself look. He saw a tall, skinny kid, with watery, brown eyes framed by dark circles. He had a dusting of dark hair on his upper lip and thick, shoulder-length hair. He had his mother's sculpted cheekbones and long, black eyelashes. Michelle had always envied him his lashes. "One day, girls will go crazy for your eyes," she'd say. "It's not fair. I should have got those, but I guess even with my stubby lashes I'm still pretty hot."

He dropped the razor into the sink and examined his arms, flexing his muscles. He'd lost a bit of weight—could do with some bulking up. With his left hand, he lifted his shirt. He pressed the blade to his skin, waiting to feel, and in a second the relief came. *Ironic isn't it? To save myself, I have to destroy myself, one small cut at a time.* He cut out the hurt, and when he had finished, he returned to his bed, took a hit of vodka, put on his headphones and lay in the dark.

Nirvana. Kurt got it.

The music surrounded him, lulled him, and eventually pulled him into sleep.

Downstairs, Bryan's mother sat for a long while at the table. She listened to Bryan moving about above her head, and she heard the drone of the newscaster coming from the den where her husband sat. She didn't have the energy to go to either of them. Finally, she took the plates and emptied them into the garbage. Then she took the rest of the roasted chicken and emptied it into the garbage, too. She loaded the dishwasher.

"I'm going to bed," she said to nobody in particular.

Nobody answered.

Five

The following evening, Bryan escaped to his room before dinner, pleading a headache. His mom's concern didn't go any further than offering him an Aspirin. His dad seemed not to care one way or the other who was at the table. In the days of Michelle, the family shared every evening meal—if you didn't participate, you'd better have a damn good excuse. Bryan took the Aspirin, even though he didn't have a headache, and opened his laptop.

This is what was going through Bryan's mind as he stared at the words on his computer screen: *People die, and then they don't talk to you anymore.*

Not ever.
Why not?

Bryan continued reading:

> *Done with the work of breathing;*
> *done with all the world;*
> *the mad race run.*
> *Through to the end; the golden goal Attained*
>   *and found to be a hole!*

"The golden goal Attained and found to be a hole!" Bryan especially liked this definition. It went beyond mere description to truth. It was from *Devil's Dictionary* by Ambrose Bierce.

He entered 'corpse' and found: *body, bones, cadaver, carcass, carrion, cold meat, loved one, mort, remains, stiff, the deceased. That pretty much covers it,* he thought.

Some people would call Bryan's interest in death another obsession. He would disagree. He would explain that in order to come to terms with death, one needed to understand it. To that end, he had spent a lot of time in the past year fooling around on his computer, trying to figure out exactly what it means to die. So far he knew this to be fact:

Dead people disappear.

Quickly.

They vanish. 'Gone' means to become extinct. To not *be*. There is one benefit to being dead: everything you've ever done wrong, every misdeed, every act of disobedience, every unkind word or broken curfew, is erased. New memories are conjured. The deceased becomes pure and good and faultless.

He knew this firsthand. After all, it had worked out this way for his sister. *Could it work the same for me? Could I be good when I'm dead? I don't want to be dead. I just want them to love me as much as her.*

Fact: Everyone has secrets. Some more than others. Little secrets, big secrets, secrets that don't even matter, and secrets that—if revealed—might be catastrophic. Your secrets die with you.

Nobody, not a living soul, suspected Michelle's secret. Poker-faced Michelle who made the Principal's List every year, but hardly studied, who could have dated anyone, but chose to date no one. Michelle had a secret, but Bryan would never tell because on the day he'd caught her, he'd promised her never to breathe a word to anybody.

Before:
She is in her room. He has called her from the hallway, but she does not answer. The music drowns his voice. It is a band he has never heard, but that does not surprise him. Michelle is always finding new bands. They always sound good. He'd like to know

who they are. Do they have a page on MySpace? So he walks into her room. She is sitting on her bed. Her long black hair shields him from her view. He is about to say something, but he sees the razor in her hand, sees it move across her upper arm. He is scared, this he remembers. He starts to back away, changes his mind. "Michelle?"

When she looks up, her eyes are unfocused. "What are you doing?" he asks.

"It's nothing. It isn't deep. It makes me feel better." Her voice seems far away. She seems far away.

He nods his head even though he doesn't really understand. "Better? Are you sick?"

"Not that kind of better. It makes me feel . . . it makes me feel . . . I don't know how to describe it." She pats the bed. "Come and sit, Bry."

And she shows him how it's done. He still doesn't get it, but he watches, and later he will think about it.

"Don't tell *anyone*," she pleads. "Nobody. Especially Mom and Dad. Swear you won't tell them. Ever. They would never understand."

"How long have you been doing this?"

"I don't know. A few years."

"But why do you do it?"

"Shit happens," she replies. "And people handle it in different ways."

Her tone implies no more questions.

"I won't tell. I promise."

"Cross your heart?"

"Cross my heart." He mimics drawing a large X over his heart.

"Hope to die?"

"Hope to die," he repeats.

She laughs, and the tension between them breaks. Together they recite:

> *Cross my heart,*
> *And hope to die,*
> *Stick a needle in my eye.*

"Now get out of here," says Michelle. "I'll see you at the sham we call dinner."

He leaves, forgets to ask her about the band. Forgets everything but the astounding fact that his sister cuts herself to feel better. Weird.

Now:

Looking back, the silly children's ditty seems ominous.

Michelle's transgression wasn't so bad. It didn't involve homicide or robbery, or money laundering or selling drugs. Her crime had been perpetrated against herself, a dirty little secret, and nothing more. Still, Michelle had been wrong when she said that nobody would understand.

Bryan understood.

Bryan understood Michelle's actions more easily than he did his parents' reaction to the death of their daughter. They spoke of her rarely and then only in hushed tones. They'd turned her old bedroom into a shrine. But they'd wiped the house clean of her photos. Mom and Dad had successfully and completely disappeared Michelle.

Yet, in spite of all their efforts, she still filled the house.

Michelle would have been twenty-one. Her birthday had come and gone without comment, without fanfare. Like the emperor who had no clothes, her birthday was marked, but not talked about. Although Mom shunned religion (upon Dad's insistence, they'd married in a civil ceremony, and had raised their children as atheists), she made some exceptions. She had insisted Bryan and Michelle accompany her to church on Christmas Eve and on

Easter morning. And Michelle's service had been held in a church. On that single occasion, Dad kept his disapproval to himself. But Bryan knew his mother well. He guessed Mom visited that same house of worship on the anniversary of Michelle's death. He speculated she'd lit a candle in memory of her lost child. There she prayed for Michelle's eternal life. She'd visit the House of God alone, hidden from Dad's mocking eyes.

"Why won't you come with us, Dad?" a much-younger Bryan had asked.

"I'm a scientist. I don't believe in God," he'd replied. "Your mother can be weak at times—or hypocritical."

Yet he'd agreed to a church service for his daughter's funeral.

For Dad, who had a scientist's mind, to be unscientific was to be stupid, and stupid was worse than anything.

Michelle had been the smart one in the family. After all, she had escaped, hadn't she?

Bryan couldn't get away from the past or from the memory of his sister or from his parents or from himself. His future looked pretty bleak, too.

Every time he went to his own room, he had to pass Michelle's closed door. Sometimes, in those first few weeks, he found himself forgetting that Michelle wasn't in there. He found himself forgetting that Michelle didn't exist anymore. He found himself forgetting that Michelle was gone.

No more Michelle—only stuff that might belong to anyone—and elusive memory.

Fact: Most people are uncomfortable with death.

They said things like: "I'm sorry to hear that you have lost your sister."

He hadn't *lost* her. She wasn't a car key or a book, or a twenty-dollar bill, or a file gone AWOL.

Why couldn't people say the word 'dead'?

He wanted a different, more honest comment:

Fill in the blank. I'm sorry your sister _____

> is dead.
> is late.
> is departed.
> bit the dust.
> bought the farm.
> fell off the perch.
> kicked the bucket.

is pushing up daisies.
got rubbed out.
went to meet her Maker.
hung up her hat.
is safe in the arms of Jesus.
passed on.
was laid to rest.
is 404.

Bryan thought back to . . . what? September '07? Two months after Michelle's death, when he found the courage to enter her room.

It is the perfect day for a reconnaissance mission—parents out, Stella's day off. Opening the door tentatively, he is afraid but does not know exactly why. Bryan steps inside and closes the door behind him. He leans back against it and surveys his whereabouts.

Michelle's room faces south. On this day, the weather is unseasonably warm and sunny after weeks of grey rain. He has grown up here, in this coastal city built on a rainforest. Yet the dark, wet days rest heavily on his shoulders. He welcomes the light.

Somebody, probably Mom or Stella, has opened the blinds and the sunlight pours through the windows. Tiny specks of dust dance just out of his reach. The air is dead: How long since a window has been opened? Everything is in its place. All there and accounted for, and yet all wrong—like holding up a letter to a mirror—all the words in their place, but jumbled, not making any sense.

Michelle's room, yet not her room. In the drawers, the clothes are neatly folded and colour-coordinated. On the left-hand side of the drawers are the darker shades, the blues and blacks and greys. Stella? Mom? The shelf above Michelle's bed is lined with childhood crap: soccer trophies, team photos, skater posters, Beanie Babies and LP covers. Michelle's brush and comb sit on her dresser, strands of her black hair (the final colour) trapped in their bristles and teeth. The bed is made; the corners are tight and tucked, the pillow fluffed, the sheets turned back.

Anger. This is not what he remembers. Where is the Michelle his father picked on but couldn't reach? The messy, loud Michelle? The sleep-in-until-2-p.m. Michelle? The fuck-you-and-leave-me-alone Michelle? Where is his sister?!

Erased.

The guitar and amp have a place of importance near the desk where the now-obsolete computer watches him with the vacant stare of a dead TV screen. An old shoebox, unmarked, sits on top of the dresser. Dust accumulates. He is drawn to the box, perhaps there are photos, but he won't know unless he opens it. He can't.

Something she said on that last night about the guitar . . . ?

I can't breathe. I think I'm going to throw up. I can't be here.

Bryan backs slowly out of the bedroom. "Never again," he swears. "Never again."

Except, he knows it's a lie. He will return to the shrine, because it is not as intimidating as he'd thought. Mom ventures into The Michelle Shrine *on a regular basis. Sometimes she cries, other times she sits very still and stares into space as if she might will her child to return, as if a little patience and a lot of grief might cause Michelle to claw her way out of the grave and come home. Mom touches the things that once belonged to her dead daughter, runs trembling fingers over her desk, picks up a book and replaces it gently on the shelf, smoothes the unnaturally smooth quilt and fluffs up the pillow. Who can guess what is on Mom's mind? Bryan can. Bryan knows all of this because sometimes she leaves Michelle's door ajar, and spying is not beneath him. He has seen his mother bury her nose in his sister's neatly folded T-shirts and gulp in her lingering odour, intoxicated, comforted by her memory.*

Later she will drink herself into oblivion.

Those are the good days.

Bryan tried to understand his mother's behaviour, but couldn't. He knew from all his research that Michelle's scent would be long gone by now. To keep everything as it once had been struck him as bizarre and spooky and idiotic. Somehow it hurt, too.

In his room, he pours himself a healthy shot of vodka and settles on his bed to listen to some Nine Inch Nails. Their lyrics describe him—stuck in time while Michelle has moved on.

Bryan knew everything there was to know about how a body decays. He had made the study of death his personal mission. He understood that, by now, Michelle's corporeal self had been reduced to hair and bone—the most horrifying stages of decomposition were long over. This knowledge served to comfort Bryan. The dead, he reasoned, are as blissfully unaware of the army of insects whose job it is to break down skin and tissue, as they are of the cold and wind and the crushing weight of the soil above their heads. Perhaps the dead are lucky. After all, Michelle didn't have to witness her own inevitable deterioration.

Not like Bryan. Bryan felt himself grow smaller every day. In time, he, too, would disappear. Mom preferred to sit alone in Michelle's room with her memories while Bryan faded away.

Funny how the parents pretend not to notice.

On the outside, we look like such a normal family.

But there are problems that outsiders cannot see. Bryan sees the problems, knows they are bothering him. He can't remember the sound of his sister's voice. He can't remember her expressions. Has he imagined the way her mouth turned up when she smiled, or was it real? Did the fine lines he thinks appeared on her forehead when she frowned really exist? Did her brow really crinkle when she laughed? All of this is lost to Bryan. He can't remember what it felt like to have a sister.

He does remember a dark road. And the rain. And the last laugh. He remembers a cold, sticky hand clutching his. Last words: "I'm scared." He remembers the deafening silence and a bloodied mannequin lying impossibly still in a pile of twisted metal.

He still hears screams.

After he came home from the hospital, he took a razor and did with it exactly what he had witnessed her do so many times. He found solace in the blade.

Who could blame him?

Six

It had been sitting untouched in a corner of Bryan's room for months now, neglected and out of tune, but now, a few nights after that horrible family dinner, it seemed to call to him. Bryan's guitar—the knock-off Fender that his family gave him for his twelfth birthday. Even though he knew he would be getting it—had, in fact, been allowed to choose it himself—that morning remained in his memory as the best day of his life. Before the Fender, there had been another guitar, one that couldn't hold a tune, but whose frets were placed closely together to accommodate a small child's hands. He had spent two years exercising his fingers, in hopes of stretching them enough to prove to his dad that a real guitar would not be a waste of money.

Of course, in his dad's eyes, any guitar would fall into the category of frivolous purchase. Mr. Bianchi would have preferred a violin or a piano or anything non-electric for his children. Michelle defied their father. She went out and mowed lawns, babysat the neighbours' bratty kids and made her own money to buy her own instrument.

"I try not to get too involved with Dad," she explained to Bryan. "It's something you might want to work on, if you want your life to be easier."

Bryan longed to question his sister further, to find out more, but sometimes Michelle could be impatient. She didn't give her time easily. Bryan tried to follow her advice, to avoid his father, to make his own decisions.

Easier said than done.

Their best times together had revolved around making music. Bryan played well, but Michelle, she had been amazing. Sometimes, before the end came on that dark, wet night, Bryan used to stand in the doorway of Michelle's room and watch her play. Her fingers moved across the neck of her Rosa Hurricane magically, playing it as if it were a human body: touching it in all the right places, slowing down and speeding up instinctively. Michelle never needed sheet music. When she had heard a song once, she claimed it as her own, changing it or adding to it until it became an extension of her personality. When she played, she closed her eyes, blocking out the rest of the world and all the shit that went with it.

It was then, that I loved her the most.

Bryan could play, but not like that. He practiced a song over and over again to get it right. He downloaded tabs from the internet, not from his own mind, and he had never mastered how to turn a good song into a brilliant one. When they played together, Michelle always led and Bryan willingly followed. That summed up their relationship—not exactly leader/follower, but something close to it.

Bryan hadn't picked up his guitar for over a year. He'd tried. All through his grade-eleven year, he had wanted to play, but every time he tried, his fingers refused to work. Last summer, he'd given up altogether. He had thought the desire to play had left him forever, but now, nearing the end of the first semester of grade twelve, his guitar inexplicably called to him. It sat on its stand, exactly where it had been when he returned from the hospital, ten hours into the nightmare that defined his new existence. And now, on this night, encouraged by the vodka coursing through his bloodstream, he felt as drawn to it as a crackhead to rock. He walked across the room, counting his steps carefully, and reached out for the guitar. It felt like an old friend in his trembling hands—mysterious, but still familiar.

Like his ex-girlfriend, Jessie—the girl he'd dumped without explanation following the accident. Worse yet, he'd done it by e-mail—too scared to do a face-to-face, knowing he couldn't pull it off while looking directly at her.

Jessie. In his mind her face was as clear as if she were sitting in front of him. Red hair, pale, freckled skin. No makeup. Green eyes, almost too big for her face. Temper. Funny. Loyal. Her image slammed into him, took his breath away. Unexpected. He tried to force her out of his head, but as usual, she did as she pleased. He'd probably never have a girlfriend again. He didn't deserve one. It had been a long time since he'd allowed himself to consider her, and for a few minutes, he gave in. He lingered over her for a moment, realizing that, for the first time in a long time, he could use a friend. *Don't want to go there.* He shoved her memory away. *Not ready for that yet. One thing at a time. And right now, it's the guitar.*

He plucked on the knock-off Fender's strings; it was terribly out of tune and the resulting twangs caused him to wince. He sunk to the floor and moulded his body around the guitar, feeling the warm wood against his mutilated stomach and the weight of the instrument on his knees. Beginning with the E string and working his way up, he brought it back to life. Softly, and without the amp, he played old songs that he thought he had forgotten and newer songs that he had been afraid to try before. He literally played himself out—out of his mind, out of his worries, and out of his fears. He didn't know how long he played, only that his wrist ached and his fingers stung, the once-calloused skin at the tips now gone soft.

Bryan closed his eyes and retreated inside of himself. Without warning, Michelle appeared; sitting across from him, her head bowed, her long, lean torso bent over her guitar, her dark straight hair covering her dark eyes, her bare foot tapping up and down in time to the music. *Dude*, she said, *You haven't lost the touch.* She gave him the thumbs-up and started to strum along with him.

Bryan smiled and kept on playing. That night he didn't cut himself. He slept. He even dared to imagine *happy*.

The next morning he felt . . . something . . . almost good. The unfamiliar emotion took him right through the early hours. He got out of bed and showered and dressed and went downstairs. "Hi, Mom," he said, reaching for the box of Cheerios, and wishing for the millionth time she'd let him eat Cap'n Crunch. He filled his bowl to the brim and doused it in milk.

"Hi, honey." Her face lit up.

How long had it been since he'd greeted her in the morning?

She poured herself a cup of coffee and joined him at the table. The coffee cup shook slightly in her unsteady grip. There were dark circles beneath her lifeless eyes and her jeans hung off her frame. She'd lost weight. When had that happened?

"You're up early."

"Yeah."

"Good, because I have an early appointment." His mother worked for a nursery, designing balcony gardens. She'd taken a leave of absence, had not been able to face work after Michelle left—spent almost a year staring at walls—before returning part time, although her heart didn't seem to be in it anymore. Bryan's father always left for work before the rest of them were out of bed. "I heard you playing last night," she added guardedly.

"Yeah. I felt like it."

She pushed a strand of hair from her face. Her nails were black, and he knew she'd already been out in the garden, watering her precious plants. "Well, that's good."

In Bryan's family they didn't talk about the important things. They talked about the weather, the news, the car, or people they knew, but not about themselves. This conversation and where it might go made Bryan uncomfortable. "I guess." He stood up, put his bowl and spoon in the sink before heading for the closet to grab his jacket. "I'll see you later."

She followed him into the front hall. He stood at the door and watched her approach him. She smiled, and her step seemed lighter. "You seem . . ." She smiled tentatively.

He cut her off mid-sentence. "Mom, leave it, okay? It's no big deal. I picked up the guitar. I got out of bed by myself. Can we just leave it at that?"

"I didn't mean to upset you . . ."

"Mom, just let it go, okay?" He exited, slamming the door behind him, his energy depleted with each word she spoke. All the way to the bus, he pictured her as he'd left her on the other side of the door—a solitary figure always on the verge of tears and the DTs.

Why does the way she feels always have to depend on the way I feel? He kicked at a stone on the sidewalk and sent it flying into the street, narrowly missing a passing car. The driver glared at him, and flipped him the finger before disappearing around the corner.

At school he didn't cut any classes. Not that it made a difference to him—he didn't learn anything either, except that the act of being there seemed to be enough for his teachers. He aced a Math test, but he excelled in Math. His teacher assumed he had studied, because otherwise she might have had to admit it was his genius and not her teaching skills (or lack thereof).

A few days later, buoyed by the jam session with Michelle and still slightly euphoric, Bryan decided to ask his mother if she knew if there were any photos of Michelle around. Where had the family albums gone? Maybe, if he could look at a picture of Michelle, even once, perhaps he might remember her face.

He didn't want to talk to Mom in the morning—he didn't want to talk to anyone in the morning; it was all he could do to drag himself out of bed and into his clothes and out the door. So he planned to leave it until after dinner one day, after Dad had disappeared into the den to watch the boring news. He would wait for the perfect moment before broaching the subject.

He didn't have to wait that long after all. Suddenly, Dad stopped coming home for dinner altogether. Mom seemed indifferent. She didn't even bother making excuses for his absence. It infuriated Bryan. If *she* didn't give a shit about anything, why did she expect him to? Bryan had always imagined that dinner without Dad would be way more relaxing, but in truth, Mom sucked as a dinner companion. By six o'clock, and sometimes earlier, she was half-tanked and pretty intense.

Three days before winter break, he worked up the courage to confront her. He'd gone over the conversation all day in his head and raced home after band practice. He burst through the front door, calling "Hi, Mom."

"Bryan." She still seemed blown away whenever he greeted her. "You're late. I was worried."

"I had band."

"Don't you usually skip band practice?"

"Most of the time, but not always. It depends on the music. Is Dad home for dinner tonight?"

"I don't know." She shrugged, setting her glass down on the coffee table. "Would you like a glass of water?"

"Yeah, like that's water you're drinking," Bryan muttered under his breath. "No, thanks," he said aloud. "But there is something I do want." He walked over to her and placed his hands firmly on her shoulders. He didn't want to touch her, but he needed to get her immediate attention. "Mom, I want to see the pictures. I know you haven't thrown them out."

"The pictures?" she repeated, stumbling over her words. She tried to shake free of him, her long, uncombed hair falling into her bloodshot eyes.

"You look like shit," Bryan said.

She flinched. "Please don't talk to me like that." She tried to wriggle away again, but he held her firmly. "Stop, Mom." Bryan hadn't stood this close to her, nor had he touched her, in a long time. Her slightness surprised him; he towered over her. Beneath his hands he felt a tremor run through her body. "Just stop and listen to me for a second." He softened his tone and released her, shoving his hands into his pockets.

"I'm sorry. You startled me. I'm listening." Her eyes darted to her drink, but she made no move to retrieve it.

"Our pictures. You know the ones you and Dad disappeared last year? All those photo albums, all those framed portraits, our school pictures, and our holiday pictures. You took them. I need to see them." Bryan took a step backward.

He hadn't intended to scare her, or to intimidate her. He left that role to his father. "It would mean a lot," he added.

"Bryan, I'm not sure you are ready to see those pictures. I'm not sure any of us are. I mean . . . your father . . ." Her words fell away.

"God, can't you for once make a decision without Dad's permission? I can hear him now." Bryan folded his arms across his chest and glared at his mother in a perfect imitation of his father. "Isabelle, we need to get on with our lives and stop moping about. Isabelle, don't you think Bryan should be on Zoloft? Isabelle, Bryan might do better in a new school. I don't think much of his friends. Isabelle, I think it might be better to put away anything that might remind us of Michelle."

"Bryan, please don't mimic your father."

"But it's true. How did Michelle put it? 'Mom's cool, but she's an invertebrate—no backbone.' You won't make a move until Dad gives you the okay." (Most people would have said 'worm' instead of 'invertebrate,' but Michelle had liked to play with words, mostly to see how others reacted.)

Mom flinched at Michelle's words. "Bryan, please don't . . ."

"Just one picture. Dad doesn't have to know. I can't remember what Michelle looked like." Bryan's voice cracked. Of course, he couldn't tell her the whole truth—that Michelle visited him on a regular basis—but that those visits were becoming less frequent, and he feared that each time she appeared would be the last time. Although tempted to confide in her, he knew she wouldn't believe him, and besides, it would be just one more thing for her to worry about. Anyway, didn't he have a right to have a photo of his sister? He swallowed and took a deep breath, fighting frustration. *Bad time for tears. She's relenting.*

Mom covered her face with her hands. "Oh, God. Sometimes I can't remember either." She paused, lowered her hands. "Okay, I'll give you a photo, but only if you promise to look at it with Doctor Kepple."

Dr. Kepple had been just one of the three psychiatrists Bryan had met during the last fourteen months. As he had done with the two before Kepple, Bryan outsmarted him in their first session together and immediately lost respect for him. No, he wouldn't go back—not even in exchange for the photo.

"Forget it, Mom. The guy's a loser. You thought so, too. Pick someone else, someone who doesn't talk down to me, and I'll go. Anybody else, just not that jerk."

And that is how he ended up—on a Friday afternoon at four o'clock—in the office of Danielle Spahic, MD, with the precious photo in his jacket pocket. Mom had kept her end of the bargain, now he had to keep his. He arrived at his appointment determined not to like Dr. Spahic, which didn't present too much of a challenge because he didn't like anyone, except of course Michelle and Jessie. Dr. Spahic's office wasn't in a building downtown or in a hospital; it was in the basement of her home, only a few blocks from his school. That would have been convenient if he had attended school that day, but he had skipped and therefore had to take the bus from downtown to get there.

He arrived fifteen minutes late, because the movie didn't end until three-thirty, but if Dr. Spahic noticed, she said nothing. In fact, she kept him waiting for ten more minutes. "I'm just on the phone. Make yourself comfortable," she called out to him.

Bryan sat down on a worn sofa in her living room. Two large tabby cats rubbed up against his feet. They pushed their pliable bodies against his shins and meowed. He petted them to shut them up, but found the sensation of their soft fur beneath his fingertips pleasing. While he touched their sleek fur, he took in his surroundings. The room was not small, but cozy. Nothing matched anything else—it was as untidy as his own room was neat. He smiled, imagining his father amongst all this random chaos, and for a second his morose expression left him, transforming his face. The bookshelves were crammed with books,

and a music stand stood in the middle of the room beside a keyboard and an electric guitar.

Dr. Spahic appeared in the doorway, a smile on her face. "Sorry
about that. You're obviously Bryan. I feel bad about keeping you
waiting. I'll stick some time on at the end if we need it or if
you want it." She shrugged. "After all, both of us are late, if you
count my time on the phone." She leaned down and picked up the
smaller of the two cats. "That was the vet. I have to take Poppins
in this evening. She isn't doing well. She's off her food." She
buried her nose in the cat's fur and sneezed. "I've been told I'm
allergic to them, but they do me a world of good."

The doctor wore jeans and a T-shirt that said: I GIVE A SHIRT. Her
dark blonde hair hung down past her shoulders. She wore no
makeup, and she wasn't very tall.

Bryan loved the T-shirt. He felt immediately comfortable in her
presence, liked her, especially looking at her through his dad's
eyes: "Totally unprofessional," Dad would sneer, or something
like that.

Poppins looked completely fine to Bryan. Fat, if anything. Reading his mind, Dr. Spahic looked up at him and grinned. "I know
what you're thinking. She's fat. But she likes to be fat, don't you,
baby?" She put the cat on the table.

"How do you know?" laughed Bryan. And then, "My dad says cats are dirty and not too smart." *Where did that come from?*

She lifted Poppins gently from the table to the floor. "I don't know how I know. I just do." She straightened up. "Your dad doesn't sound like the most charming man."

"He's not," agreed Bryan. "Actually, he can be a real A-hole."

"Come on," she said. "Let's get comfortable and we can talk some more."

He followed her down a short hall that led to the back of the house. The office was in even more disarray. "Take a seat wherever you are comfortable."

Bryan looked around. There were four large, comfortable chairs, all covered in a mish-mash of material. Books, files and papers filled every chair and another music stand stood in the corner under the large bay window. "Where do you sit?"

Dr. Spahic lifted a pile of books off the most tattered chair and placed them in two random piles on the floor. "Right here."

Bryan moved some books off a second chair and sat down opposite her, so that he could see out the window into her garden. Before he sat down, he evened out the two piles of books she had made. He thought she might say something like, "Sorry about the mess," or "Don't touch my books," but she didn't and he liked her for it.

They stared at each other for a minute. Bryan waited uncomfortably for her to speak. When she didn't, he shifted uneasily in his chair. He cleared his throat and he looked everywhere but into her green eyes.

"I'm sorry," she said finally. "I'm making you uncomfortable. I don't mean to at all. It's not some weird doctor trick. I was just gathering my thoughts." She picked up a file folder from the floor. "I actually have all your information here, but I'm not sure where you would like to begin."

"I don't have a clue. Isn't that kinda up to you?" Bryan goaded.

"I suppose it could be, if you want it to be." When Bryan didn't reply, she continued. "Since this is our first meeting, and since I get to be the boss, I think we will just talk—you know, get to know each other. Normally, I like to record our sessions. I hope you don't mind, but it helps me to remember what was said after you've left. I'm sure you know the routine?"

Bryan nodded. *Oh, yeah, I know it well.* So far, it was the only thing that had happened since he entered this house that hadn't surprised him. "Whatever."

He had expected that, like all the other shrinks, the informal chat would quickly turn into a formal session. She would shoot prying questions his way and make him analyze pictures. They would play retarded word-association games, and she wouldn't be able to hide her shock at his contrived-to-shock answers.

Wrong.

For over an hour they sat in the dwindling light and talked about all sorts of things. Bryan found out about her cats. She played both the keyboard and the guitar. Her real office was being renovated, and so she had agreed to take a few select patients in her own home. He couldn't guess her age, and he didn't really care. When the session was over, he left reluctantly.

Bussing home that evening, he thought about the picture of Michelle tucked safely, and still not looked at, in his jacket pocket. He thought back on what Dr. Spahic had said about the whole thing. "I don't really understand your parents' reluctance over letting you have a photograph of your sister, but in the end, your mother did provide you with one. You know, it's perfectly normal that we forget the faces and the voices of the people close to us who have died. When I spoke to your mother, she was adamant that we look at the photo together. How do you feel about that?"

"I'd rather look at it on my own, if you don't mind."

"Of course. As I would, if I were in your shoes. We'll talk about it the next time we see each other, okay?"

"Yeah, but I don't think the parents will be too happy about me doing this on my own."

"Only tell them if you want to. Everything that goes on here is confidential. Don't forget, Bryan, it would be very strange if you remembered every physical detail about your sister, after so much time has passed. And even if you did," she added, "you have every right to a picture of your sister."

So. She understood.

"Next time," she said, "the real work begins. That is, if you think you're up for it."

In retrospect, it had almost been a good day, but good days were fleeting. The next morning he woke up to the old, familiar blackness. In less than a week, it would be Christmas.

He dreaded it.

Seven

Christmas, as Bryan had anticipated, had been a complete disaster. He'd gone through the motions, as had his parents, but nothing more. As expected, Mom made a superhuman effort to make it as it had been, but Michelle's ghost cast a pall over the house. Very few people dropped by. No big surprise there. Dad went out of his way to make it clear that he considered the whole holiday to be a waste of time and money—he'd always felt that way about Christmas. But in the past, they'd managed to ignore him, and enjoy themselves.

Right up until a few days before Christmas, Bryan hoped that they'd ignore the whole celebration, let it pass, like they had at Thanksgiving. It almost happened that way, but at the last moment, Mom caved and brought home a small fir tree that she'd picked up at the school Christmas tree sale. It leaned at a precarious angle in the corner of the living room, its sad branches shedding needles on the floor. "Some tree," Brian commented.

"Come on, Bryan. Help me decorate," she pleaded, doing her best to get into the spirit of the holidays.

"Sure. Whatever." Bryan retrieved the boxes of Christmas decorations and lights from the attic and plonked them on the living room floor. It took several trips up and down the stairs, and while he worked, his mom poured herself a large glass of wine, watching him silently, her earlier enthusiasm gone. *Who's helping who?* he thought. But when he opened the box containing the carefully packed handmade decorations, he understood her sudden mood change. "Damn, Mom. I can't do this."

They stared down at the child-like decorations nestled in the box—some Michelle's, some his—all lovingly crafted through the years of elementary school. One for each Christmas of Michelle's young life. Neither had the heart to put them on the tree. They brought a flood of memories of years past, when there were four in the family, not three. Mom started to cry. "I'm sorry," she said.

"Yeah—me, too," Bryan shrugged and closed the boxes. Then he carried them all back upstairs to the attic. The tree-decorating party had come to an end.

Still, he and his mom went to the local church, just like they had done every Christmas for as long as Bryan could remember, except that for the second year in a row, Michelle wouldn't be with them. Dad stayed home as he did every year and watched *Charlie Brown's Christmas* on TV. Bryan knocked off half a bottle of vodka before they left for the carol service. At church they lit a candle for Michelle and didn't sing when the rest of the congregation did. After the service, his mother hung back, shaking hands and chatting with people who were clearly uncomfortable seeing her. Bryan stood on the sidewalk, smoked a cigarette and thought about how his world had changed.

You suck, God.

He spotted Jessie and her sister and mom and dad—stupid to forget that they would be here. He turned away when she waved at him. He couldn't face her. He'd treated her so badly, and yet she'd waved at him as if nothing had happened. He knew he looked terrible; black circles framed his bloodshot eyes, his hair hung limply to his shoulders. The last thing he wanted was for her and her family to see him like this. So he turned away, hoping to lose himself in the crowd. Still, Jessie managed to find him.

"Merry Christmas," she said, approaching him slowly. "Bryan, how are you?"

He said nothing, only looked down uncomfortably. He waited to see how she would respond to his hostility.

"I've e-mailed you. You don't reply. You never reply."

"I don't have much to say these days." He shrugged. "Do yourself a favour and get a new friend."

Jessie's eyes teared up. "So, it's like that, is it?" She made as if to walk away, then angrily turned to face him. "What did I ever do to you? When did you become such a jerk? Michelle is gone. She's *gone*, and that's not my fault. It's not your fault, either. She did it to herself. Lucky she didn't take you along with her. When are you going to get a grip?"

"Fuck you, Jessie. You want to know how I am?" He grabbed her arm roughly and pulled her away from the streetlamps and into the shadows. He unbuttoned his jacket, just about to expose the shredded skin on his stomach, until he realized what a mistake that would be and stopped himself. "Suffice to say, I'm not doing well at all," he snapped. "And that's all you need to know. Why don't you just go back to your happy little life?"

Jessie reached for him, but when she touched him, he shook her off. "I don't want sympathy. I just want everyone to leave me alone." He felt hot—feverish—and the words rolled out of his mouth in slow motion.

"You've been drinking," she accused.
"Not enough," Bryan retorted.
"You're a complete jerk," she said through tears.

"Yup. I'm a cold-blooded son of a bitch." In the corner of his eye, he saw her parents approaching. Jessie's parents were okay, but he couldn't face them, not now. "Merry Fucking Christmas," he said, scowling at her, and disappeared into the night. Mom would have to get home without him.

But he felt their eyes on him. Always being watched...His teachers' eyes, his parents' eyes. His shrink's eyes. Strangers' eyes. Dead eyes. He felt them now, hundreds of eyes watching his retreating back—Jessie, her mom, her dad, her sister, his mother, the minister and all of those God-fearing strangers. They stood there outside the church in the dying year, and tried to figure out what part of his tangled personality they were personally responsible for, and what portion of the blame belonged to him.

Eight

Stella ran warm water over the mountain of dirty dishes spilling out of the kitchen sink onto the sticky countertop. Then she loaded the dishwasher with yesterday's lunch, last night's dinner and this morning's breakfast plates, cups, utensils and pots. Bits of dry food clung to the knives, forks and spoons, leaving her no choice but to scrub the cutlery first. It was inconsiderate for them to have left the kitchen in such disarray. Inconsiderate, but not surprising these days. "Thank goodness," Stella said to herself. "I can get out of here as soon as this is done. And, hopefully, before they get home."

She paused, chewing on her lip, remembering a time when she had loved her work here, had even felt a part of the family. Rightfully so, considering she had been with the Bianchi family for a very long time; she had come to think of it as her own. Her fault, really, she mused—after all, she should never have mistaken being treated well for love. Yet, Isabelle had always been a fine person to work for, not demanding, not bossy, but pleasant, almost a friend—at least she had been, but not anymore. The husband had always been a bit difficult—unfriendly and set in his ways— but she'd been able to work around him. And the children? Stella squeezed her eyes shut to hold back tears. She'd loved Michelle with all her heart, and now Michelle had gone to live with Jesus. She loved Bryan as if he were her own son, but he had put up an impenetrable wall between himself and the rest of the world, and the more she tried to break it down, the higher it got. "I gave up on him," she whispered to herself. "But what choice did I have?"

From where she stood at the sink, she could see through the kitchen window to the backyard and the beautiful garden Isabelle had grown and nurtured with such care. Thinking about Isabelle and the garden brought a smile to Stella's face. Gardening seemed to be the only activity Isabelle could bear anymore and the one thing that she still derived pleasure from. She'd done it alone last year. Now, in March, Stella saw the garden springing to life again—soon the tiny green shoots pushing through the soil would be two feet tall or higher, topped by bright flowers of every colour and description. The cherry blossoms were already in full bloom and the branches of the apple tree—naked last week—were sprouting bright leaves. Only the little vegetable garden that belonged to Bryan and Isabelle remained untouched. It lay at the bottom of the garden, unkempt. Stella pictured Bryan and thought how a neglected garden, like a neglected child, cannot flourish.

She finished loading the dishwasher and wiped down the counters, checking the houseplants that lined the windowsills as she worked her way around the room. They were bone dry. Before she lost her daughter, Isabelle would have never let this happen. Stella watered each one, taking care to only dampen the soil of the cacti as Isabelle had taught her. In the past, when the family had gone away on vacation, it was Stella who watered the plants, brought in the newspaper and collected the mail, but she doubted there were any holidays in this family's future—not when they couldn't bear to be in the same room as each other for even a few minutes.

Stella grieved for Michelle, and she understood the pain the Bianchi family felt, but she believed that, at some point, they needed to start living again, to look forward and not back. If they did not learn to do this, then they would crush Bryan. In a strange way, his deceased sister had become a stronger presence in the house than he was. Stella wanted to take his parents and shake some sense into them. After all, they still had one child and their tears were drowning him, sure as if they'd dropped him off a boat in the middle of the ocean and sailed away.

There would be no point in talking to the father. He was a cold man, and she was slightly afraid of his intimidating presence. But she'd have to talk to one of them soon. Bryan was getting worse. It wasn't just the drinking and cigarettes anymore. She knew he'd been hurting himself in another way—a shocking way that she didn't understand, but it frightened her more than anything. She'd thought about confronting him with the evidence, but couldn't figure out how to do that without destroying the limited communication they still shared.

So, she would just have to stand by helplessly and watch them self-destruct. It was because of this that she had become so silent and so removed, especially from the boy to whom she had once been so close.

When she'd told her best friend about what Bryan was doing with the razor, Lily hadn't believed her. "No way," she'd said. "You're making it up."

"No, I'm not," protested Stella, "I've looked it up, and it's God's truth. Some people do this, usually girls."

"You have to tell his mother," Lily scolded. "She is a friend to you."

Stella blinked back tears. "*Was* a friend. Now she is my employer. Besides, even if it were different, I couldn't tell her—couldn't take the risk of Bryan finding out. If I betray him, he will have nobody."

"It's not betrayal. What if something happens to him? Whose fault will it be then? You have a responsibility."

"Let it go, Lily. I will do what I can when the time is right." Lily let it go, but Stella knew her friend thought her a coward, and because she couldn't explain herself more clearly, the unresolved conversation had driven a wedge between them.

"Too much reflection," she thought, but as she put on her coat and stepped out into the warm evening, Lily's words haunted her. Maybe her friend had a point. Maybe it *would* be her fault if something happened to Bryan. "I will talk to Isabelle," she promised herself. "When the time is right." She locked the front door behind her and, deep in thought, slowly walked to her bus stop.

Nine

Bryan continued to attend school, but only sporadically. He was a good student—brilliant some of his teachers said—so his absences didn't influence his marks, only the way his teachers saw him. Point blank: when he'd started high school, they'd had lofty hopes for him. He'd been a good student, an A student since grade eight and, up until Michelle's accident, attendance hadn't been a problem. These days they didn't like him. They complained about his chronically empty seat and in the staff room, away from the ears of parents and students, they called him arrogant and waited for something to 'pull him down a notch.' Secretly, horribly, some had hoped tragedy might do the trick, and when it hadn't, they disliked him even more.

Bryan had lost count of the number of times he'd sat in the hard wooden chair in the principal's office. His mother would sit beside him in the more comfortable seat reserved for parents and other important people, which was anyone who didn't attend the school as a student. She would wring her hands nervously as the principal listed off Bryan's latest transgressions: swore in class, skipped class, wore MP3 player in class, rude to teachers, called another student an idiot, and on and on. She'd always defended him, even when there was no defence—which Bryan thought had to be the worst thing in the world. "Mom, I hate it when you do that. I know I eff up. School is boring. Teachers are boring. I can learn in a day what it takes most kids a month to learn. My marks are really good. I'm on the Principal's List every year. Most of the kids are stupid, and you sound pretty lame always taking my side when I don't have one. I wish you'd back off or at least give me one good reason why I should be at school every day."

She'd tried, tried to find one good reason, but failed. They'd all tried. Nothing worked. Not detentions, not threats of expulsion or pleas to his conscience. That one always cracked him up.

Conversation overheard between his father and his mother the previous week:

> Mom: "I was at Bryan's school again today."
> Dad: *"Now* what?" (Bryan doubted he even looked up from the six o'clock news.)
> Mom: "He called his Math teacher . . . well let's just say he called her something he shouldn't have. Oh, and he's missed a lot of school lately . . . again."

Dad:	Silence followed by heavy sigh.
Mom:	"They've been trying to go easy on him because of . . . you know . . . because of what he's been through."
Dad:	"They're not doing him any favours. Bryan needs to toughen up. He can't live in the past forever. Half of the problem with that boy is the way you all treat him like a baby. People have been through worse and you know it, Isabelle. How many kids will die in Iraq this year? Are all of their families going to fall apart?"
Mom:	"That's not fair."
Dad:	"Fair? Neither is life, Isabelle, and you, for one, should know that. Now, if you don't have anything else to say, I'm in the middle of the news."

End of conversation. Mom leaves the room. Sound of door closing.

Bryan, halfway down the stairs at the start of this conversation, decided to avoid his mother. He retraced his steps to his room and shut the door quietly. Dad's indifference and anger, Mom's sadness—all his fault. For a week, motivated by guilt, he attended class every day, even Phys. Ed. The next week, he found it difficult to keep up the perfect attendance charade, and by week three, he found the whole thing unbearable.

I'm done, he thought as he entered the looming front doors of his school, one minute after the final bell had rung. Kids still crowded the halls in a last-minute rush to get to their first classes on time. Bryan, never at ease in a crowd, waited for the flow of bodies to pass by him. He'd be late and that meant he'd be in shit, so why bother picking up the pace? School sucked, but how to explain this to the people who wielded the power—his teachers, his parents and their team of mental-health workers who listened without hearing?

Of course, he admitted to himself, it wouldn't have sucked quite as much if Jessie hadn't switched schools and if he hadn't screwed up so badly with her. "Stop," he said to himself. He'd done a good job of blocking her out of his thoughts for almost two years, but every so often, she reappeared, uninvited and unwelcome. When that happened he couldn't pretend to himself that he didn't miss her.

As fate would have it, Bryan's locker, located on the third floor, couldn't be farther away from his first class, located in the basement. His feet felt like concrete as he ascended the stairs. He moved slowly, like a prisoner on his way to execution. When he was almost there, he realized he'd left his homework on the desk in his bedroom. Things couldn't get much worse. Or so he'd thought until he got to his locker. Some clowns had put a lot of effort into telling him—in black spray paint and pointed language—exactly how they felt about him.

Something new here. He didn't have any friends—the friends he had, like his old life, had disappeared when Michelle left. No, he didn't have any friends, but, as far as he knew, he didn't have any enemies either. Probably some stupid ninth-graders acting on a dare. Ignoring what had to be someone's idea of an intelligent prank, he spun his combination lock, overshooting the last number. He failed again on the second try. *Shit.* He dug his hands into his pocket and pulled out a painkiller (*thanks, Mom*), to ward off the headache beginning to gnaw at his temples. It had to be a sign, so instead of trying to open his locker again, he turned around and headed for the nearest exit.

He heard the *click-clack* of heels on tile—someone was approaching. He thought about making a run for it, in case it was a teacher, but then thought better of it and slowed to a halt. One minute he had been alone and carrying on a conversation with himself and the next Mrs. Ward, the school principal and bearer of all things bad, stood behind him, her hand clamped on his shoulder. He spun around and shook her hand off. *Damn. Why do people insist on touching other people?*

She took a startled step back at his hostile reaction to her touch. "Bryan, I didn't mean to frighten you. I thought you heard me behind you."

"I did, but I was kind of lost in thought."

"I can see that. Is everything okay?"

Ah, the million-dollar question. In spite of all the evidence, they always have to ask it.

"Yeah, I'm good. A little tired, but good. Things are okay. School is good. Everything is good." Bryan turned his lips up into the shape of a smile. "Really good. Up late doing homework . . . you know how it is." *God, she must be a complete idiot not to see through this.*

On his last visit to Dr. Spahic, he'd said, "I keep the real me buried. Nobody wants to know that guy. People ask me stupid questions all the time, and usually I just tell them what they want to hear."

"For example?" Dr. Spahic asked.

"Okay, say, like they ask: 'Did you have a good day at school?' And I answer, 'Yeah, it was great!' And I nod, as if I had the best day any human could ever have had, as if I'd won a million dollars, as if my dad had just presented me with a brand new hot car, as if . . ."

"Okay." Dr. Spahic grinned. "I get it. And then?"

"And they're like, 'excellent,' and then, when they believe me—and they always do—I lose total respect for them. It's a joke, man. Except that, half the time, I don't even know what I'm really feeling or who I am, so it's a pretty lame joke."

Dr. Spahic giggled, and when Bryan shot her a puzzled glance, she said, "Sorry, but you have to admit it is a bit of a joke, when people act that way."

Bryan leaned down to pat the cat rubbing up against his ankle. He smiled.

"Don't let Poppins bother you. Seriously, though, don't worry. You're in there somewhere—the real Bryan. It's just a matter of finding you."

"Yeah, I get it. Except, I'm not sure if I want to be 'found.'" He'd smiled, for the second time in less than an hour.

><

"... and I'm glad to see you can smile about it. We all know what a busy year grade twelve is. Drop by my office if you have any concerns. I like to think I'm always available for my students."

Bryan shuffled his feet. She'd been talking the whole time he'd been daydreaming. "Ah, thanks, I will."

"Good. Now you'd better get going or you will be later than you already are for your first class." She looked at her watch pointedly. "Off you go."

Bryan retraced his steps to his locker, sure she would keep him in her sightline. She'd be suspicious if he just sauntered off to class without books. Or maybe not. After all, she hadn't noticed his newly decorated locker, or that he hadn't heard a word she'd said. Still, the close encounter left him feeling cold and clammy, and the combination lock shook in trembling hands. Spin twice to the right. Twelve. Back to the left. Twenty-four. Full circle. Forty-eight. Bingo! He popped the lock and peered inside. Disaster—books in a disorganized pile at the bottom of the locker, candy wrappers, an old tuna sandwich, a rotten apple, dirty gym clothes, including running shoes and socks. The smell turned his stomach. *Maybe Stella would agree to come to school and clean out my locker,* he thought wildly. He laughed, too loudly, and the classroom door directly behind him slammed shut. He closed his locker, and hurried down the hall empty-handed to his English class.

He wanted to sneak in unnoticed but failed. "Nice of you to join us," Mr. Green sniped.

Bryan ignored him and dropped into his seat. The stupidest kids giggled while the rest waited. Bryan knew they were easy to entertain, but that role didn't appeal. What he really wanted was an invisibility cloak. He glared at Mr. Green. "My pleasure," he spat. "I would rather shoot myself than miss a single one of your erudite lectures." His classmates held their breath in unison. They sensed bloodletting. Shakespeare was to be delayed.

"What did you just say to me?" Mr. Green stood up and picked up a piece of chalk. Bryan hoped he might throw it at him—a chalk bullet.

"I said, I'm sorry I'm late. I missed my bus this morning." The words rolled out of his mouth slowly. He was in a movie and watching it at the same time.

The chalk snapped in half in Mr. Green's clenched fist. "Not a problem. You can be the first to read your piece on *Hamlet.*"

Bryan checked for his books. He looked on the floor, he looked under his desk, and he opened his jacket and pulled out a pack of cigarettes. "Not in there," he said. Mr. Green watched him silently, ignoring the occasional snort or giggle from another student. "I thought I'd put them in my shoe," Bryan laughed. "Sorry. Not funny. I think I left my books at home. Not to worry." He slouched down in his desk and muttered, "*I have lost all my mirth . . . the earth . . . seems . . . sterile.*"

"I didn't catch that. Could you speak up, please?" Mr. Green's voice sounded as if he'd swallowed glass.

Bryan stood. He kicked his chair aside, threw back his shoulders and faced Mr. Green.

"I have of late—but wherefore I know not—lost all my mirth, forgone all custom of exercises; and indeed it goes so heavily with my disposition that this goodly frame, the earth, seems to me a sterile promontory, this most excellent canopy, the air, look you, this brave o'erhanging firmament, this majestical roof fretted with golden fire, why, it appears no other thing to me than a foul and pestilent congregation of vapours."

"Sit down, Bryan."

"In a minute." He turned to face the class. "Listen up!"

"What a piece of work is man! How noble in reason! how infinite in faculty! in form and moving how express and admirable! in action how like an angel! in apprehension how like a god! the beauty of the world! the paragon of animals! And yet, to me, what is this quintessence of dust? man delights not me: no, nor woman neither, though by your smiling you seem to say so."

Bryan bowed and sat down slowly. No one said a word, but everyone watched as Mr. Green's loose fleshy cheeks turned from white to red to crimson and finally purple. Just before he self-destructed, he moved his bulk (surprisingly quickly for a man of such girth) from behind his desk and crossed to where Bryan stood. Bryan counted out each step in his mind. *One, two, three, four, five.* Not a good sign. If only he were seated a row back, if only he were nearer the door, or drunk, or anywhere else in the world. If only he were dead. *One more step,* he bit his tongue wanting to yell, *Make it six!* Already the cards were stacked against him.

He stood to meet Mr. Green. *"What a piece of work is man,"* he repeated, his eyes fixed on his teacher's dark stare.

Everyone watched and waited. He felt their cruel little eyes on him. Bastards. Bryan folded his arms across his chest. *"What a piece of work is man,"* he shouted. "No truer words were ever spoken! That is my paragraph."

Mr. Green stopped in front of Bryan. He took a deep, deep breath and unclenched his fists. He took a step back, and Bryan could almost hear him thinking, *I won't lose my career because of this little jerk.* "Very nice," Mr. Green sputtered. "Appropriate and true. However, your outburst does not constitute a paragraph. I have no doubt that if I asked you to continue, you could, and would, quote the whole of *Hamlet* without hesitation. But I didn't ask for that, did I? I asked for a paragraph. A simple little paragraph." Mr. Green looked like a raptor looming over his prey. Bryan stood very still. "You have no books with you. You are late for the third day in a row. Perhaps you would like to visit the office, again." When he said the word 'again,' spittle flew out of his mouth. Bryan watched the tiny drops evaporate in the sunlight streaming through the windowpanes.

"I'd like to change seats," he said. The words spilled out of his mouth before he could stop them, but he felt better. He'd told the truth. He grinned up at his English teacher. "I'd like to change seats," he repeated, louder still. "Would you have a problem with that?"

The assholes in desks twittered. He swallowed the hate he felt for them, but it caught in his throat like a fishbone so that he couldn't breathe. Couldn't speak. He thought he might pass out.

Control.

"No. You can't change seats. If you are not here to learn, I don't want you in my class. My job is to provide an education. I'm not a prison guard and this is not a prison. This is a learning institution."

"Not true," Bryan retorted. "I have been on time every day this week. I have been present every day for the last three weeks, but I haven't learned a thing." His stomach turned and he wanted to be sick. "But to answer your question, sir, I would like very much indeed to leave this room. If you need me, I'll be in the office . . . again. And by the way, when you talk, you spit."

CUT

The applause began before he'd left his seat, and it rose to a crescendo as he slammed the door behind him. The classroom had erupted, and Bryan felt certain Mr. Green had erupted as well. He tore down the hall, vaguely aware of the shouts and taunts following him. He ran, not even bothering to count his steps—down the staircase, out the door, and onto the street. He crossed the road blindly, hoping a car might plough into him. No such luck.

To be killed seemed a most difficult thing.

Ten

As he neared his stop, a bus approached. Another minute and he would have missed it, would have been forced to wait forever for the next one, or walk. He didn't mind walking, but he hadn't worn a warm jacket and the spring air still carried a bite. His mom wasted a lot of breath always telling him to dress more warmly, but today, if she'd bothered, she would have had a point. She'd been asleep when Bryan left the house at 8:25 a.m.

"Bryan, I'm going to sleep in today," she'd called to him, her voice sounding more like Janis Joplin's than his mom's. "Take some money out of my purse for your lunch."

"Sure, Mom. Happy Hangover." He took a twenty-dollar bill out of her purse, not because he needed it, but because it pissed him off that she always lied about why she slept in.

The bus lurched to a stop beside him, and Bryan pulled out his pass and dove through the doors, moving quickly down the aisle in search of an empty seat. Tiredness, his new companion, walked beside him, and the thought of standing proved too much. Feeling both preoccupied and distracted, he dropped into the first empty seat. He decided that without a destination in mind he'd ride until he felt like getting off. He patted his jacket pockets, thinking it might be a good time to really zone out, listen to some tunes, but he realized he'd left his MP3 player on his dresser that morning. He slumped against the cool window-glass and sighed. Great, now he'd have to listen to his own thoughts all day.

The morning rush wasn't quite over. Office workers on their trek downtown sat quietly either reading, listening to music or staring vacantly out the windows. Bryan liked watching commuters—especially the ones who looked like they'd just climbed out of bed. Often, to pass time on the bus, he'd make up stories about their lives. He'd just begun to pick a protagonist—the guy with the dreads and the cell phone stuck to his ear—when he felt a soft tap on his shoulder.

He looked back into green eyes; the green eyes he'd been trying so hard to block out of his mind for months. "Hey, Bryan. Long time, no see."

Bryan gulped. "Hey, Jess. 'Sup?" He knew he'd turned crimson—he felt the colour crawling up his face.

"'Sup? That's all you can come up with after all this time? Anyway," she shrugged, "I'm good. You?"

He shifted around in his seat and stared at her mutely. She didn't seem the least bit awkward or uncomfortable, even though he had been an asshole to her at Christmas. He looked down at the rubber-matted floor, strewn with litter. "Uh..."

"How's school? I don't miss it a bit, not for a single second. Your hair is really long." She kept talking as if he wasn't acting like a complete flake or a total idiot. "How's the family? Still messed up?"

He grinned in spite of himself. "Pretty much." She'd always been able to cut through the crap, until almost the very end. Even then he'd held onto her words the same way he'd held onto his baseball cards from years ago—possessively, revisiting them when he felt the need. "Yeah, the parents are pretty much screwed." He stopped smiling because she didn't smile, and because it wasn't funny, not really. True, but not funny. Still, lying to Jess had always backfired on him. He swore she could read his mind. Long ago, he'd decided to either tell her the truth or shut up. He couldn't see any reason for a change of tactics at this point. He'd both loved and hated her for being so perceptive. "Yeah," he repeated, "Screwed is the best word I can think of to describe them."

Her expression remained neutral. She listened to him intently, and then she sat back in her seat and appraised him. He tried not to blush as her eyes studied his face. He tried not to notice the splash of freckles across her nose, or the length of her eyelashes. "You look like shit," she stated matter-of-factly. "Really, though, how are you doing?" She also hated small talk. As far as he knew, she hated him, too, so why the friendly attitude? You couldn't trust anyone anymore. Not even the girl who used to be your best friend. Not even the girl you'd hurt for no reason at all.

He ignored the second half of her question, instead concentrating on the easy part. "Yeah. I look like shit, and thanks for pointing it out. I hadn't been aware. Things are going. I'm working part time—selling knives door to door. Dad seemed to think I needed to be gainfully employed."

Jessie laughed. "I can hear him now: 'When I was your age, I had two newspaper routes. Blah blah blah . . .'"

Bryan laughed. "Yeah, well. So far I haven't sold a single knife. Still, it shut the old man up. Ironic, isn't it?"

"Ironic? What do you mean ironic? I don't get it."

He'd almost blown it. He'd let his guard down. "I don't know why I said ironic. And you? What's it like going to university?"

"You could have skipped a year, too, Bry." There was a sadness in her voice that hadn't been there a second ago.

"I know it." He dug up the courage to look at her directly. She looked good. Her eyes were as he'd remembered them: green and almond-shaped and dead honest. Her hair, whose colour he couldn't name but might be a shade of red, hung down her back, braided in a hundred different strands. A heavy silver chain fell around her neck.

He wondered if she'd kept the bracelet he'd given her on her last birthday. He wondered about the belly-button ring (he'd gone with her to have it done), and the little raven tat on her upper left arm. "Why a raven?" he'd asked.

"Because ravens are smart and they're tricksters, and I like that," she'd answered.

An open book sat on her lap, but he couldn't make out the title. She wore her trademark black low-cut jeans and, like him, a black tee, but her piercings were all wrong. He counted nine in all—three rings in one ear, four in the other, and two studs in her nose. No good. "You should get another earring," he suggested—"you know, so your ears are even."

"Jesus, Bryan. You've been spending too much time watching reality shows. I'm happy with my piercings. Besides, maybe you should spend a little more time on yourself and a little less time telling me what to do."

"Yeah, you always had a problem taking advice." He shrugged.

"Yeah. And you always had a problem giving it when no one has asked you for it."

"Whatever." Bryan suddenly wanted to be away from her, but as if she were reading his mind, she reached out and touched his arm.

"Bryan, I don't want to fight. Believe it or not, I've missed you . . . even though you can be a prick."

He pulled his arm away. "Don't miss me, Jess. Nothing's changed. I'm good on my own." He looked around wildly, wondering how close they were to the next stop, but Jessie beat him to it. She reached up and pulled the cord for the next stop.

"Yeah, I can see you're really good on your own," she retorted.

"Look, I'll get off here. This isn't your stop, and I'm not going anywhere."

"Truer words were never spoken." She paused. For a second, Bryan thought he saw her confidence waver. As the bus rolled into the stop, she shoved her book into her bag and turned to him. "I know you want to make me hate you, but I won't. You hate yourself enough for everyone. See ya. Call me if you ever decide to be a nice guy again."

Bryan shook his head and, while he thought about a response, the doors swung open and Jessie hopped off. Swallowed by the city. Another disappearing person. For once in a very long time, he actually cared.

When the bus pulled away from the curb, he sat very still, looking straight ahead. It took a huge amount of effort for him not to jump off the bus and chase after her.

Eleven

He didn't even bother to pretend he hadn't been in school that day. Eventually, his mom would find out, and all hell would break loose when that happened, so why delay the inevitable? Besides, with luck they were all out, and he didn't feel like wandering the city streets aimlessly anymore. He hopped off the bus, crossed the street and hopped on one going in the opposite direction, arriving home around 11:30 in the morning.

He let himself in the front door and, obeying his rumbling stomach, headed straight for the fridge. He'd just settled down in front of the TV with a grilled-cheese sandwich, when he heard the front door open. Seconds later, Stella entered the room. She didn't see him at first, and when she did, she gave a startled little cry. "Bryan, you scared the life out of me. I didn't expect anyone would be home."

"Sorry about that. I thought the house would be empty, too. I forgot you'd be here."

"You haven't come home for lunch since you were a little boy." She put down her purse and removed her coat. "It's cold today. Remember, you would only eat peanut butter and banana sandwiches and they had to be fresh. I let you cut the banana, because you were very particular about the size of each piece." She smiled at him. "Sometimes I miss those days."

"I'm not exactly home for lunch," Bryan replied, uncomfortable with her nostalgic look back. "I'm just home." He saw the worried look on her face. "Chill, I won't let Mom know you saw me. You don't have to get involved."

Stella pulled up a footstool and sat down in front of him. Bryan didn't like the proximity, but Stella had loved him, so he forced himself not to recoil. "Honestly," he said. "It'll be our little secret."

She looked at her arm and plucked an invisible hair from her sleeve. "I don't care about what your mother thinks, or what she says, for that matter." She coughed nervously. "Actually, I'm glad to get this one-on-one time with you." When Bryan didn't reply, she continued. "I know you've had a tough time since . . ."

Bryan held up his hand. "Don't go there," he snarled. "Just don't go there." He picked up his sandwich, thought about taking a bite, and put it down again. "Please."

Stella took a deep breath and tried again. "What I meant to say is that . . . you, you've always been my family. I'm here if you ever want to talk. I'm here like I've always been. I could talk to your mom if you like. I could do something, if you'll let me."

Bryan shifted in his chair. He wanted to be angry, to push her away, to deaden the sound of her voice. He'd already had to deal with Jessie, and that had sucked him dry. But Stella wasn't Jessie or his mom or his dad, or one of his stupid teachers. He stood up. "I'm okay," he said. "And I appreciate what you've said." He headed toward his bedroom but stopped at the foot of the stairs and turned around. "Thanks, Stella. I mean it. Thanks."

When Bryan left the room, Stella sat very still for a long time. She folded her arms and thought about the past, and sometimes she smiled, and then she remembered. After a while, she got up and went into the laundry room and organized the piles of dirty clothes into colours and whites. "I'm not giving up on him," she vowed to herself. "I hope he knows it now."

That night at dinner, Mom didn't tell Dad about Bryan skipping classes. She didn't say a word about it to Bryan either, although he'd heard her on the phone with his counsellor, so he knew she knew. "I'll talk to him," she'd promised, but she hadn't.

As usual, Dad pressed him for information about his day in a pathetic attempt at making peace. Bryan felt under assault as he deflected the endless, pointless questions: "How was your day? What classes did you have? Who did you eat lunch with? Blah blah blah . . ."

Finally, to shut his dad up, he offered a tidbit of information. "I saw Jessie on the bus."

"Oh, Jessie. How is Jessie?" His mother, suddenly perking up, broke her silence. "It would be lovely to see her again." Jessie had always been a favourite of Mom's.

Dad's reaction was totally predictable. "Jessie? Oh, I remember her. She looked like a walking pincushion. I don't even want to think about what she'll look like when she gets older. Does she still dress like some kind of creature in a Dali painting?"

Well, Dad, she doesn't like you either.

That pretty much ended all the dinner conversation. The three of them finished their spaghetti in silence. Bryan had three helpings, unable to sate his appetite. "Slow down," said his mother. "You'll make yourself sick."

"I'm really hungry. It was good. Thanks, Mom." He stood up, picking up his plate to carry to the dishwasher.

"Not so quick, pal." Dad wiped his lips, then slowly folded his napkin in a perfect rectangle, running his finger along the crease as if it were a military uniform. "Since when we did stop saying 'May I be excused from the table?' in this family?"

"Since about a year and a half ago," Bryan replied. He *felt* rather than *saw* Mom withdraw into herself.

"Sit yourself back down and ask to be excused." His father threw his napkin down beside his plate. "We're not barbarians. Your mother worked hard to put this meal together."

Bryan sat. "Actually, she didn't. Stella did. I know because I was here."

His mother gasped. "Don't," she whispered.

"What do you mean, *you were here?* How could you be in two places at the same time?"

"I wasn't. I went to school today, for about a second, and then I came home. And before you ask why, I did it because my English teacher is a jerk."

His father continued. "My boss is a jerk. I don't quit my job. You give up too quickly. You have to face the music in life, or else you may as well just lie down and die. The best advice my father ever gave me, and I'm passing it on to you is——" Bryan joined him—" 'Don't let the bastards get you down.' " His father's eyes flashed in anger.

Bryan rolled his eyes in response. "Heard it before, Dad."

Mom stood up and began to clear the table, as if she couldn't get out of there fast enough. Dad turned on her. "This is all your fault. Did you know about this?" Her silence answered his question. "You've always let him have his own way, ever since he was a baby, and a fat lot of good it's done him."

He would have kept going, but she cut him off mid-sentence. "That's enough. How can you expect him to be reasonable when you are so *un*reasonable?"

Bryan watched and listened for as long as he could. *And people wonder why* I'm *so fucked up?* When he'd had enough, he pushed back his chair and stood up, hands pressed over his ears. "Shut up. Both of you, shut up." He groaned and ran out of the room, taking the stairs to his bedroom two at a time.

Twice that evening, his mother ventured upstairs and tapped on his door. "Bryan, do you need anything? Bryan, are you okay?" *There it was again, the inevitable question.* Twice he ignored her. Finally, they went to their separate beds, and the house settled back into an uneasy silence.

While the parents slept, he cut himself twice, one slice for each of them. He went deeper than usual. It felt good. In the old times, Bryan reasoned, doctors were always bloodletting—sticking leeches on their patients so they'd feel better. Same result, different method.

After the initial rush had passed, he dug around in his sock drawer, for his emergency stash of vodka. He'd pretty much killed the bottle under the bed last week. Either that, or Stella had found it and chucked it. He took a few hits and waited for the alcohol's numbing effect. Then he put on his headphones and collapsed on his bed. Nine Inch Nails' "Hurt" rolled around in his head, lulling him to sleep.

He slept in. He meant to. He hadn't bothered to set his alarm. Mom's serrated voice shredded his dream. "Bryan. Get up! You'll be late for school. Bryan, I'm not going to call you again. Do I have to come up there?"

Fuck. He checked the clock. He'd slept for nearly twelve hours. It felt like two. He pulled on yesterday's jeans and T-shirt. He brushed his teeth. He checked his new cuts for infection—none. He grinned wolfishly at the bleary, red-eyed boy who stared back at him in the mirror. He gave himself the finger. He moved like a robot. When he got downstairs, Dad had already left for work. Mom sipped a cup of coffee. She didn't say a word, just handed him his lunch, but as he left the house, she called after him, "Don't forget you have an appointment with Dr. Spahic after school today. Four-thirty."

The timing couldn't have been better. He'd been considering his options.

He didn't have many.

Twelve

Dr. Spahic sat on her oversized chair with her larger cat, Kody, curled on her ample lap and listened attentively to Bryan as he related the events of the past week, his tone expressionless, his eyes glued to a spot somewhere over her right shoulder, But when he mentioned Jessie, she stopped scratching Kody's ear, placed the cat gently on the floor and perked up. Poppins, curled up on the chair next to her in the bottomless sleep exclusive to felines, lazily opened one eye, as if she sensed her heightened interest. Their session was almost over, and Bryan's foul mood from last night hadn't improved. They'd gotten nowhere. In truth, he'd spent most of the time thinking about getting to the music store before it closed at six. He'd snapped a guitar string last week and had only decided to replace it today.

Kody didn't like being dumped on the floor. She sat at Dr. Spahic's feet, glaring up at her, tail swishing, ears flat. Bryan liked the big tabby, although it had taken her a long time to trust him. Last week, for the first time, she'd jumped onto his lap, and it had been hard to hide his pleasure at her sudden change of heart. Up until then, she'd been very aloof, although she'd deign to sit on the footstool and stare at him unblinkingly, as if she could read all of his thoughts. He'd found it unnerving at first, until Dr. Spahic explained that that was Kody's way of deciding if she trusted him. "Her name is actually Kodiak," Dr. Spahic had said during their first session. "She isn't light-footed like a kitty; rather she saunters like a bear, but Poppins and I call her Kody for short. She's a good cat, but the shyer of the two of them, so if she joins us, we have to really welcome her."

"Sorry, Kody," Dr. Spahic purred, "but I think we're onto something here." Eyebrows raised, she looked at Bryan. "What do you think? I mean, you've talked about this girl, Jessie, before, but never in much detail and whenever you mention her name, your expression changes."

"She's just a girl I knew. I guess she was sort of my girlfriend, but I dumped her. End of story."

"Okay. Just curious. Let's move on. We don't have much time left." She took her left elbow in her right hand and pulled it across her chest in a long stretch. "I'm a bit stiff," she said. "I've been trying to build my strength by lifting weights. It's not going too well."

Bryan pulled his eyes off Kody and glowered at her. "You're not much of a shrink, are you? You just want to drop the whole Jessie thing? Just like that?"

"Well you're not much of a patient," she replied, but not unkindly. "How would you like me to respond?"

"At least you could ask me some questions about Jessie, if you think she's part of my problem."

"What kind of questions would you suggest I ask you, Bryan?"

"You could ask why I dumped her, or how I met her, or something." He stopped and leaned forward in his chair. "Okay, I get it, I know what you're doing. I'm not a complete idiot you know. Actually, I'm pretty smart."

"I know you're smart and I'm glad you realize it. It's one of your many first-rate characteristics." She glanced up at the old clock that hung lopsided on the far wall.

Bryan followed her eyes. "That clock drives me nuts," he said. He got up and wove his way through the piles of books and randomly placed furniture until he was beneath the clock. "Why'd you hang it so high up and so crookedly?" He stood on tiptoes and reached up, straightening it. "That's better," he said. "Hope you don't mind."

"Not at all. Thank you. We've got a couple of minutes left. Normally, you could stay longer, but I've got people coming over for dinner tonight, and I'm a terrible cook. I need lots of time to create a meal, burn it, and start all over again, and maybe even order in pizza after." She grinned.

Bryan sat down again, shoulders hunched, eyes on the floor. "My dad would hate that," he said. "He hates waste. Anyway . . . Jessie is super smart. She's seventeen and she's in first-year university. She skipped a grade. She's a math wizard. I could talk to her about stuff . . ." He swallowed the lump in his throat before continuing. "She's super smart, and she deserves a good guy, but she could never figure that one out, so maybe she's not so smart after all. She was, like, always wanting to be my friend, even when I was being a jerk. That's about it."

He reached over the distance between them and patted the still-sulking Kody on her fat orange head. She spun around and hissed at him, claws extended, eyes yellow with rage, before diving under the couch for cover. Bryan withdrew his hand quickly. She hadn't scratched him, but she'd hurt him none the less. "Stupid cat. I thought she liked me."

Dr. Spahic shrugged her shoulders and smiled. "Kody's a funny cat," she said. "She had a tough beginning, and it takes a long time for her to trust people. Even then, she finds it difficult. She likes you, Bryan, but if you show her any affection, her claws come out, and she runs in the opposite direction. I'm hoping one day she'll realize that she should stop hiding and let the people who care about her love her." She looked at Bryan pointedly before picking his jacket up off the floor where it had fallen and handing it to him. "I think maybe you'll understand Kody better than most."

Bryan looked into Dr. Spahic's kind eyes and realized he'd found an ally, a person he could trust. He nodded slowly. "Hope your dinner works out," he said. At the door he turned back to her. "Thank you. I shouldn't have said what I said because the truth is you're a good shrink, maybe even a great one."

That evening, after her guests had left, Dr. Spahic returned to her office to write up her patient notes. When she came to Bryan's file, she wrote for a long time. Finally, she put down her pen and sat very still, lost in thought. She had an extraordinary affection for her young patient, and she knew she had reached him on some level. But she'd sensed his desperation and it frightened her. She knew, both intuitively and professionally, that she had much to accomplish with him, and she feared she had very little time.

Bryan missed the guitar store by two minutes. The clerk had just flipped the OPEN sign to CLOSED. Bryan knocked on the glass, but the guy ignored him, so after a while, he gave up. He'd been pumped to go home and make some music, but not anymore. He didn't want to deal with his parents, either. The time with Dr. Spahic had been intense, and he wanted to think about it. He'd liked the cat analogy, except that it meant he'd really screwed up with Jessie and now he couldn't fix it.

That little conversation about Kody had stirred up a whole bunch of questions and no answers. Michelle had a role to play in all this, but what? One thing for sure, their family hadn't been this screwed up until she left.

She didn't leave, man. She died, the loud voice in his head told him. *You're worse than the rest of them. You can't even say the word.*

And he hadn't told Dr. Spahic about the cutting. She knew about the drinking and the smoking, and she was aware of his fixation with numbers, but he hadn't said a word about the way he loved to carve himself up in his spare time. If he told her, she'd give up on him, and who could blame her? Plus, he'd been lying by omission for so long that she'd never trust him again.

A car full of kids drove by, music blaring, and jolted Bryan out of his head. He didn't know how long he'd been standing on the sidewalk in front of the guitar store. He hated how he lost time so easily. He started walking without knowing or caring where he was going. He sauntered north down Alma Street past the boutiques and shops and cafés. He blocked out the elaborate window displays that hinted of summers around the corner and summers gone, and the enticing aromas from the cafés that implied warm meals and cozy restaurants where people who had friends talked to each other and held hands and discussed books. Instead he kept his head down and his eyes on the sidewalk—grey and cracked like the sky above. He shoved his hands deep into the pockets of his jeans and pulled his hoodie over his head; it was his own version of an invisibility cloak.

When he was a kid, he and his mom had played a game together. He'd stand in front of her and cover his eyes. "Where am I?" His little body would tingle with excitement, because he just knew she couldn't see him.

"Where are you?" she'd call back. "I can't see you anywhere, but you sound as if you are in the same room as me!"

He knew she couldn't see him, yet he sensed her presence right in front of him. "I'm invisible," he'd bellow. Finally, when he thought he might explode with excitement, he'd uncover his eyes. "Here I am, Mommy. I was in the room with you the whole time!" And she would scoop him into her arms and cover him in kisses. Michelle used to tell him Mom faked the whole thing, but he never believed her. As usual, Michelle had been right. Except that now he was older, and the game was real and not fun, and he didn't even have to cover his eyes to be invisible to the world.

He felt hot wet tears on his cheeks and swiped at them angrily. Too much thinking. He began to walk without purpose, down the hill, still heading north, counting each step he took, to block the images crowding his mind.

When he reached the beach, he had a choice: go west toward the university, east toward downtown, or straight out to sea. He chose east. His father worked at the university and running into Dad had about as much appeal as getting his chest waxed. Or he might run into one of the goofy grad students who inexplicably looked at Dr. Bianchi as some kind of god. So, he turned east, toward downtown.

Others strolled the beach, or stood to watch as another day, tired and worn, and cloaked in brilliant reds and oranges, sank into the horizon. Dusk brought out the romantics, the joggers, the dog owners and the lonely. Bryan stuck to the shoreline, preferring to wade through the sand and circle around the thick brown kelp, rather than dodging the cyclists, skaters and Rollerbladers who acted as if the seawall had been built for their own personal use. Every so often, he'd pass another shore-walker. Some nodded, but most, he surmised, were wandering, like him, in their own world of pain. He welcomed the isolation. He realized he hated being alone in a crowd. It spotlighted his seclusion.

As the sky darkened and dusk turned to night, the seawall emptied, allowing Bryan to abandon the shoreline for the easier concrete sidewalk. His legs were tired, so he stopped a couple of times to sit on one of the wooden benches that lined the seawall. He smoked a little, walked a little, and his anxiousness decreased. He thought he might be able to manage home. The benches had been erected in memory of the dead. Dead people, dead dogs, dead cats. Soon there would be a bench for his sister, but the waiting list was long. Bryan could see his mother and father sitting on the bench, not talking to each other. He shivered. Each bench had a brass plaque commemorating the life of a disappeared living thing. He sat down and wondered whose bench he'd occupied. The epitaph read:

In Memory of Daniel Joseph Tuner
1964–1985
Music, when soft voices die, vibrates in the memory

He liked that. He hoped somebody might write something like that for him when he died. It would depend on who chose the words—not his father, he hoped. Maybe Dr. Spahic would do it? But how could he ask her without her freaking? Who was Daniel Joseph Tuner, who had died at twenty-one? What colour was his hair? Had he been tall or short? Had his friends called him Danny or Dan? Had he left behind a girl with a broken heart? Had she found somebody else? Did he die in an accident, or had he been ill? Had he taken his own life? Had his death surprised him and those around him, or had it been anticipated? Had Dan/Danny/Daniel bargained with God at the last second? Had he discovered, as he drew his last breath, that words were a waste of time? That all those words just fell on deaf ears?

Thirteen

Time. Bryan figured he had too much of it on his hands. Memories insisted on flooding back to him, and it wasn't always easy to see the line between the real and the imagined. Thoughts, like colours, turn to mud if improperly mixed.

Dr. Spahic had said, "Don't worry. Let the memories come and then let them go," but that was easy for her to say, when the only thing she had to worry about was whether her cats were fed and inside before dark.

The Michelle memories were the hardest ones. She hovered around him, not speaking, but always present. She wanted something from him, but what? Bryan tried, but failed, to remember. He'd started to refer to her as his 'Dark Angel.' "Go away, Dark Angel," he begged, but she did not reply.

He'd taken to hanging at the beach on an almost-daily basis. He'd go there after school and stay until late in the evening. Things were deteriorating at home between Mom and Dad. Bryan hated their fights, but on the flip side, the more they fought with each other, the less they hassled him.

He sensed rain and quickened his pace. The damp wind cut through his thin jacket. If he hurried, he might just have time to reach one of the food kiosks before the sky opened up. He could do with an order of hot, salty fries to warm him up, but when he arrived at the kiosk, he realized he couldn't face talking to anyone, so he settled on a cigarette instead. He pulled out his half-empty pack of smokes. TOBACCO IS BAD FOR YOUR HEALTH screamed the label. *I'll second that*, thought Bryan, thinking not of his lungs, but of the burn marks he'd inflicted on himself. He thought of the small perfect circles on his arms that branded him as a nutter, a wacko, or whatever.

The first time Jessie had seen his bare arms, she'd recoiled, horrified. "My God, Bryan. What the hell . . . ?" She grabbed his arm and studied it carefully. "You, my friend, are definitely fucked up." She dropped his arm and took a step back, her eyes never leaving his. "I'll stick by you, but you need help. If it wasn't so stupid, it'd be cool, but it's not, it's dumb. Hey, is my name on your arm?" she added, her eyes dancing.

He'd pulled down his sleeve to cover his arm. "You're one of

two people who know about this, and all you can do is crack
a joke?"

"I'm sorry, but I mean it, you need to get some help." She put her
arm around him, but he shook her off. He didn't want to stop,
and he didn't want help, and so she left him.

Well, maybe that wasn't fair, he realized, looking back on the
whole thing. She hadn't exactly abandoned him. He'd push her
away, and she'd come back, and he'd push her away again, and
she'd return, until she finally couldn't do it anymore. She'd cried
when he told her to get lost, and even though he wanted to brush
the tears from her cheeks, he hadn't, and she'd stormed away. "I
never want to see you again."

There, she'd said it, just like he knew she would. Sure, she re-
tracted her statement in an e-mail the very next day, but she
had said it, hadn't she? He'd been right; not even his best friend
could stand him.

Bryan crushed his cigarette under his heel. The rain had come,
but it didn't matter. He continued walking, trying to expel all
thoughts of Jessie from his mind. Tough to do. He walked quickly,
keeping his head down, oblivious to the rainwater dripping into
his collar and down his back. He paid no attention to the ocean,
or the mountains to the north or to the people he passed. He just
walked, but he could not stop the noise in his head.

Eventually he tired and made a beeline toward the next unoc-
cupied bench. He sat down heavily, every bone and muscle in
his body exhausted. *I feel like I'm about ninety years old.* It didn't
matter how much he slept at night, it never seemed to be enough
anymore. He leaned back and looked up at the black clouds. He
felt the rainwater wash over his face. He stuck out his tongue,
like he used to do when he was a kid and tried to catch rain-
drops. He spotted a lone gull, and watched as it scavenged for
food, swooping and diving above the sand in search of anything
edible left behind by humans. Bryan admired its aerodynamic
beauty, its healthy size, and its ability to survive in the big city.
He wished he could fly like that.

Fly away.

And then he remembered something about seagulls. A lot of people didn't like them. Dad, for example, really had a hate on for the
opportunistic, cheeky birds. The whole family used to picnic at
the beach when he and Michelle were kids. Bryan remembered
how Dad used to coax the gulls over with lunch offerings so he
could gain their trust—and then he'd find ways to hurt them.

Prick.

One time he got a gull so bad—heaving a rock at it—that he
broke its wing. Man, his mom was *pissed*. She just got up and
walked away, muttering under her breath. Michelle followed

her, but when Bryan tried to go after them, his dad called him
'wussy' and 'wimp.' "You stay here with me," he ordered. Bryan's
arm hurt where his dad held him in his iron grip.

Remembering:
He hands me a stone. A small round stone, the kind with lines
on it that you wish on.

"Throw it. Go on."
"No. No, Daddy. Uh-uh." I will disappear. He is so angry. I want
Mom.
"I told you to throw it. Bloody gulls. Scavengers. Stop being such
a baby. Your mother isn't here to protect you."

"No."

Don't let him see my hands shake. Poor bird. Don't cry. He will
kill me. I am somewhere else. I am with Mom and Michelle. I
am invisible.

"Bryan, do as you are told. Hit that bloody bird, or I'm going to
leave you here by yourself."

Daddy never raises his voice when he yells at me. He gets quieter,
but scarier.

"Don't go, Daddy. Don't leave me here!"

" 'Don't go, Daddy.' You sound like a little girl."
"I feel sick. Don't kick sand at me. It hurts my eyes. It's not funny. Mom!"

"If a bad man takes you away, it will be all your fault, cry-baby."
"No, Daddy. Don't leave me."

But Daddy is leaving. His tree-stump legs are moving across the hot sand. He is laughing, but he is not pleased. His eyes are cold. He is leaving me here alone. Sand and tears. "Daddy, come back!"

"Wait for me!" The sand is hot, burns my feet. My eyes hurt. Stop wiping my eyes with sandy hands. Hot sand. Don't let anything bad happen to me. Here, by this log, curled against its warmth I am safe. I am invisible. I see the stone. It is perfectly round and there are no wish lines on it.

The stone fits. No more crying. Come back. I will throw the stone at the bird, but you can't leave me. Quiet now. Shhh. Missed.

"Stupid bird. Mommy?"

Be angry. I don't care. She is here now. She asks, "What do you think you are doing?" She asks, "Where is your father?" "Stop crying," she says. "Stop clinging."

Michelle takes my hand. She pulls me away from Mommy. She pulls me to where the waves lick the sand, and I put my toes into the water. Michelle crouches beside me and folds me up in her arms. "Bry, you have to stand up for yourself."

Michelle's hand is warm. The ocean is warm.
"Bastard," says Michelle.
"You said a bad word."
"You say it now. You'll feel better."

"Bastard," Bryan mumbled, as the curtain dropped, and the memory receded as quickly as it had come. "Wow," he murmured. "That sucked."

By this time, he was soaking wet, miserable and tired; still he didn't want to go home, not when he felt as grim as he did. That memory, from so long ago, had jolted him badly. He got up, shook himself like a dog and headed down to the beach, slogging through the wet sand, until he reached the shoreline.

He couldn't see a soul for miles. A pair of ducks bobbed up and down on the whitecaps, and a group of gulls huddled together on the wet sand. The angry clouds shrouded the mountains to the north, and the rain beat down on him. He'd never felt so alone in his life.

Fourteen

Burrard Street Bridge is one of the many bridges that separate Vancouver's downtown from its residential areas. Bryan had crossed it often by car, but he had never done it on foot. The narrow sidewalk offered no barriers or fences to separate the pedestrians from the cars, trucks, and motorcycles whizzing by. Worse yet, those on foot had to share the sidewalk with bikers and people on Rollerblades. Twice, Bryan bumped into people, and the second time he almost fell off the sidewalk and into the traffic.

There seem to be all sorts of ways to off myself, he thought, *but that's not what I want.* It took focus to walk across the bridge, and he didn't have a huge store of that.

Beneath him was the marina. To his right was the Granville Street Bridge, and below that, Granville Island, the high-end market, perched on the waterfront. It would be teeming with shoppers and tourists and noise and colour. Bryan continued over the Burrard Street Bridge, where jumpers were common enough that they didn't even make the headlines. Every so often somebody in the gently rocking boats below him risked witnessing a body plunging from the air above to the water. Bryan felt a sense of hopelessness descend on him. He looked away, hurrying now. Once he'd crossed the bridge, he followed Burrard Street, past the movie theatres, past the hotels and expensive boutiques all the way to Robson Street, where he turned right toward the Granville Mall.

Before he'd been born, the mall had been a busy downtown street, a vibrant retail area. His parents talked about it often, about how much better it had been before it had been closed off to traffic. They complained about the 'riff-raff' that populated it now, and Mom hoped it would one day return to what it had been. Dad swore that would never happen, because it would be a political decision. "All politicians are assholes," he said. "All they ever do is raise my taxes and make empty promises."

Dad had a real thing about how his taxes were spent, or misspent.

Bryan didn't know what had drawn him to the Granville Mall. His parents were right. It was a decidedly seedy strip of downtown Vancouver, though not the worst. That distinction belonged to the Downtown Eastside, a patch of the city nearer the waterfront. Still, there was little that Granville Mall had to boast about. Apart from a few trendy clothing stores, fast-food restaurants and convenience stores lined the street, separated from each other by pubs and nightclubs. The stench of garbage and sickness hung in the air. Above the business establishments, hookers, drug users and transients frequented run-down, filthy hotels. Some of the city's largest movie-theatres and playhouses vied for space with some of the city's seediest establishments, and because of this the Mall attracted both Vancouver's poorest and wealthiest citizens.

In short, Granville Mall was an ideal place for the down and out, for panhandlers, drug dealers and petty thieves. Street kids flocked to the mall in droves, attracted by money, drugs and booze, but mostly by the companionship they found there. Bryan wandered down the sidewalk. He stopped to listen to a busker picking at his guitar. The guy had talent, so Bryan tossed a couple of bucks into his guitar case. "Thanks, dude." The busker nodded at him from behind hooded eyes. Bryan shrugged. The guy played well, and it wasn't much money.

I could probably make some good money out here if it ever came to that.

There were a lot of kids his age hanging on the street. He felt a mixture of intimidation and excitement at the sight of so many kids surviving on their own. He stopped at the corner of Smithe and Granville and smoked a cigarette, taking in the streetscape. A guy busied himself digging through an overflowing garbage can, popping other people's discarded food into his mouth. Bits of newspaper stuck in his matted, blonde hair, and a thin trickle of blood wept from an open welt on his cheek. Bryan wondered what his story was. He didn't look that old. He started to create the guy's story in his head, but didn't get far before a kid who looked to be about his age approached him.

"Fixated on the Walking Germ?" He laughed. "He's harmless until he freaks. You got an extra smoke by any chance?"

"Sure." Bryan reached into the pocket of his jeans and pulled out a cigarette. He handed it to the kid, who took it gratefully.

"Got a light?" Bryan handed him his lighter. The kid's hands were black with dirt and shaking; it took him a few tries to light the cigarette. He didn't say a word until he had taken three deep drags on the cigarette, and then he handed back the lighter. "Thanks, man. You're not from around here, are you?"

"Not really. You?"

"I am now. Originally I'm from Toronto. I heard this might be a better place to spend the winter. Lotus Land and all that shit, but I hate the fucking rain. Goes right to the bones. How do you stand it?"

There were all sorts of questions Bryan wanted to ask the boy but instead he stuck out his hand and said, "I'm Bryan."

"Chris." He clasped Bryan's hand, his skin cold and calloused to the touch. He'd bitten his nails to below the cuticle, and they were encrusted in dirt. His hand shook uncontrollably as he shifted nervously from foot to foot.

"How about a burger?" Bryan offered. They were standing opposite a McDonald's. His dad always told him to never give bums anything, but if you had to give them something, offer them food, not money. Besides, the dude looked like a skeleton.

Why should I give my hard-earned dollars to a lazy beggar? He can get a job like anyone else. Nobody gave me any handouts.

Shut up, Dad.

"I'd rather have cash. The fix I need has nothing to do with food."

Bryan pulled out a fiver and stuck it into Chris's hand. "Sure, man. Whatever."

Money is plentiful where I come from.

"Wait here, man." Chris took off at a trot. He disappeared around the corner and into a back alley. Bryan didn't expect to see him again, didn't really care, but he reappeared minutes later. "Got some ice. Come on. I'll share."

"Come on, where?"

"Just away from here. The cops are everywhere."

Bryan hesitated. This was out of his comfort zone, but at the same time, he liked Chris, so he shrugged off his doubts and followed his new acquaintance down the street. It felt good to be included, to not look or feel like an outsider. Chris darted into a back alley where the stench of garbage and urine hit Bryan hard. He covered his nose with his hand. "God, this is bad," he said.

"You get used to it," Chris mumbled, distractedly. "Especially with a little help from this." He held up the small plastic bag, filled with tiny chopped-up crystals. "Asshole ripped me off," he fumed. "Hey, Bro, spare another smoke?"

"All right." Bryan handed him another cigarette.

"Cheers." Chris stuck the smoke behind his ear. "All set," he explained. He searched through his pockets, pulling out old butts, torn paper, a pencil stub and half a cookie. Finally, he found what he was looking for—a carefully folded rolling paper. He devoured the cookie, then crouched on the filthy pavement, took the cigarette from behind his ear and went to work emptying the tobacco onto the rolling paper. He mixed some of the crystals in, but try as he might, his hands shook so much he couldn't roll it. "You do it, man. I'm amped. But be careful. Don't effing spill any."

Bryan rolled the 'cigarette' and handed it back to Chris.

"Your lighter." He lit it and inhaled deeply. "God, I needed that." He closed his eyes and smiled, before taking another hit. "You," he said, holding it out to Bryan.

"What is this shit?" Bryan sounded more confident than he felt.
"Speed."
"Speed?"
"You deaf? Straight up. Speed. Ice. Crank. Come on, man. Crystal meth. It's the real deal. Guaranteed to transport you. Guaranteed to make this crap world a better place."

"No, thanks. It's yours." Bryan handed it back to Chris, who took it greedily.

"Whatever. Just means more for me." He waved the cigarette in front of Bryan's face. "Take it or leave it."

Bryan studied Chris closely. He knew all about meth. Who didn't? He knew it could really fuck you up in more ways than one. Chris's eyes had glassed over, but the tension Bryan had seen in his face earlier had disappeared. He looked relaxed. "One time won't hurt you," he coaxed.

When he smiled, Bryan recoiled. Chris's breath smelled like he was rotting from the inside out, but it was the teeth that scared Bryan. The few Chris had left were stained or black. One hung at an awkward angle, barely anchored to the red, swollen gums. "Jesus," Bryan said. Chris didn't hear him. He'd escaped the street for a while. He had a dreamy look on his face. Bryan almost took the meth. He wanted to feel good for once. He wanted it because he was tired of being laughed at. He wanted it because he didn't want to look like a fool. He wanted it because he didn't want to offend Chris. He wanted it because it had been a long time since he had a friend, and Chris seemed to be a pretty friendly guy. He wanted it for all of those reasons.

Bryan took out his smokes and put a twenty-dollar bill in the pack. He shoved it into Chris's clammy hand. "Good luck, man," he whispered. Chris struggled to keep his eyes open, to focus on Bryan. "No," he said. He handed the cigarettes back to Bryan. "I don't need these, but will you stay with me? Just hang here with me for a bit?"

"One hit," Bryan said. "Just one."

"That's all a newbie needs."

Bryan inhaled, and the anxiety that had become his only companion slid away. "It's all right," he said.

"Yup," agreed Chris.

They stood together, not talking, smoking cigarettes.

And Michelle was there.

Fifteen

"Wake up, man. We gotta make a move. Cops and everything. Can't stick too long in one place."

Bryan was in his own world. He felt a little sick and his heart was racing. He opened his eyes. He looked around for Michelle, and saw Chris grinning at him. "I think I had a dream," he said.

"Yeah, sounds about right. Bet you're not hungry now." Chris laughed. "First time's the shit. Come on, man. Let's walk and smoke."

Bryan fell into step beside him. He felt totally energized, as if he could keep on walking and talking forever. Everything around him, the tall grey buildings, the street lamps, even the blackened dumpsters seemed beautiful, and the intensity of colour was amazing. As darkness settled over the city, lightness settled on Bryan. When Chris suggested scoring some more meth, Bryan handed him another twenty-dollar bill. "Get some pot, for me."

"You're a regular bank machine," grinned Chris. "Done. Wait here, man."

Chris disappeared for a while and came back with a bigger baggie, and a single joint. Bryan took the joint and stuck it in with his cigarettes. "I don't need anything else today."

Chris did most of the talking, which suited Bryan just fine. For once he didn't feel obliged to make conversation or to answer prying questions. Chris knew how to stay under the radar of the cops, he knew who to avoid on the streets and who to trust. He didn't trust a lot of people. "They're no good," is how he put it. Bryan didn't argue.

Bryan didn't want to say too much about himself. Compared to Chris, his life seemed a bowl of cherries. Chris had been on the streets for almost a year, and he had good reason for running away from home. He didn't know his real dad, and his stepfather sounded like a monster. He beat up on his mom and on Chris, but Chris's mom refused to lay charges against him or to get a restraining order. "She just drinks her pain away," he told Bryan. "We used to drink together, but I couldn't stand how she got all teary."

The first few times he ran away from home, they sent the cops after him, but after a while they stopped caring. "I think my step-father liked it better with me out of the house," Chris said with a shrug. He'd spent the summer on the streets of Winnipeg, and then came west with a buddy as winter set in.

"Where's your buddy, now?"
"Dead. OD'd."
"Sorry, man."
"Why? It's not your fault." Chris laughed. "What about you? What's your story?"

They were sitting on a park bench near Stanley Park. They'd smoked the joint a while ago and were coming down from their high. Bryan felt cold and tired and ready to go home. Behind them, the predawn sky had turned a brilliant pink. "I don't have a story," he said. "Not like yours anyway. My dad is a jerk, and he gets a little rough sometimes, and my mom is okay. She's just weak."

"Doesn't sound so terrible to me," Chris slurred. "I mean," he gestured around him, "this is pretty terrible, living out here, but it beats my home."

"My sister is dead," Bryan said. "Now everything is fucked up. I don't think my parents will stay together. They liked her *way* more than they like me. She had everything going for her— brains, personality, looks."

"Not your fault, man." Chris stood up and sat down again. He got more and more jittery as the night wore on. "I'd like to go home to a warm bed right now."

"It's *all* my fault," said Bryan, in a cracked voice. "But I don't want to go there." He thought about asking Chris home with him, but he could imagine his parents' reaction. "What happened to your teeth, man?"

Chris brought his grimy hands up to his mouth. He felt around inside for a bit. "I don't know, man. Everyone gets it. Methmouth. Some side effect apparently. Is it bad? I haven't looked in a mirror for eons. They hurt sometimes."

"Not so bad. It's four-thirty. I got to go home." Bryan stuck out his hand. "I'll see you around."

Chris shook his hand. "You know where to find me, Bro." He lay down on the bench, curled into a ball and began to nod off. "If I'm still alive, I'll be on the Mall." He closed his eyes, effectively dismissing Bryan. Bryan stood for a moment, watching him, before he took off his leather jacket and laid it over Chris.

"See you around."

It took almost two and a half hours for Bryan to get home on foot. He'd been walking for half an hour, when he realized he'd given away all of his cash. No cab for him. No bus for him either—he had forgotten to buy a new pass. Three quarters of the way home, he could hardly put one foot in front of the other. His body felt numb. Although he could see his breath in the air, he didn't feel cold, only tired. So tired. As he made his way back across the bridge, the early morning commuter traffic increased. He walked as quickly as he could, too tired to bother to count his steps. Buses full of sleepy-eyed office workers rolled by, spewing black diesel fumes. Some of the people he passed on the street stepped off the pavement to avoid him, so he knew he must look pretty bad. Not so long ago, he'd felt confident and strong, now he felt exposed and afraid. His mouth tasted terrible and his throat hurt—probably because he'd smoked a pack of cigarettes—and his clothes were filthy. He thought of Chris, asleep on a bench and wondered how he stood it. *Oh, well. Not my problem. I've got my own shit to deal with—like what am I gonna tell Mom if she's around?* It would help if he knew her schedule, but routine had gone out the window after the accident.

He hadn't expected to see both his parents' cars in the driveway. In fact, he'd taken his time to ensure Dad would have been long gone to work by the time he got to his house. He rubbed his eyes, like a little kid, and looked again. *Yup. Two cars. One black sedan, one blue station wagon. Things didn't look good for him.* He snuck around to the back of the house and let himself in through the back door, taking care to be as quiet as possible. They were both there at the kitchen table.

"Where have you been?" his father thundered, before Bryan could close the door behind him. "Your mother has been sick with worry. I'm late for work." He crossed the floor in three long strides and grabbed Bryan roughly by the arm. "No coat. And you look like hell."

His mother rushed to him and threw her arms around him. "Thank God you're safe." She burst into tears.

"Stop babying him." His father shoved her out of the way. "Where the hell have you been, Bryan?" Keeping a tight grip on Bryan's arm, his father pushed him back so he could study him. "No jacket. Bloodshot eyes. Smell like an ashtray. Where were you all night?"

Bryan tried to wriggle out of his grip. Not possible. "Let go of me. And to answer your question, I was nowhere."

"Yeah, and nowhere is exactly where you are headed and fast by the looks of it." All Bryan wanted to do was to get away, but his father held him in a vice grip. "Listen to me, you little shit." He was so close Bryan could feel his hot breath on his face. "You get your ass upstairs, you have a shower, and you go to school. We'll talk tonight. Go on. Get out of here."

The whole exchange took less than twenty seconds. His mother had not moved since his father had pushed her, but now, summoning all of her courage, she stepped forward and in an icy flat voice, she hissed, "He's safe. Leave him alone. He's safe. That's all that counts. I can't go through this twice."

Bryan looked at his mother in shock. Dad looked like he'd just been poked with a stun gun. "I mean it," she said, enunciating each word, "Leave. Him. Alone."

"Leave him alone . . . or *what*?" Bryan's father said, enraged. They all held their breath.

"Just leave him alone." She collapsed at the table and began to sob, her shoulders shaking, her head buried in her arms.

Bryan stepped away from his father. "I'm not going to school." He backed up slowly, and when he reached the table, he put his hand on his mom's shoulder and squeezed it softly. "It's okay, Mom." He faced his father. "Fuck you."

Way to go, little brother.

Bryan smiled. He didn't feel afraid anymore. Mom's shoulders stopped shaking beneath his hand. She'd stopped crying.

"What did you say to me?" Dad's mean little eyes flashed. He clenched his fists at his side. "Did you just swear at me?!"

Bryan swallowed, afraid he might throw up. His breath came in short stabs. "Yeah," he said. "Yeah, I think I *did*." And it felt pretty good. Bryan smiled lopsidedly, flashed a look of reassurance in his mother's direction and walked slowly out of the room. His dad stood rooted to the spot, shock written all over his face. Bryan took the stairs two at a time, and when he got to his bathroom, he slammed the door and locked it behind him, before emptying the meagre contents of his stomach into the toilet bowl.

Behind him, his father's fists flailed against the bathroom door. Bryan prayed the lock would hold, that the door wouldn't suddenly bust open. Finally the pounding stopped. "You'll regret what you said to me. Nobody, and especially not you, *ever* talks to me like that." He heard his dad's footsteps retreating. "I'm going to work, but you better be here and ready with an explanation when I get home tonight. And you're grounded, for a long, long time."

When he'd gone, Bryan finished vomiting, then turned on the shower, took off his stinking clothes and immersed himself in the hot water, where he stayed for almost thirty minutes. Then he towelled himself off and pressed his ear to the door to make sure his father had really left. He couldn't face him again, not feeling like this. He could hear the muffled sound of his mother crying softly downstairs, but he felt only annoyance. Why did she always have to overreact to everything?

He listened until he knew for sure he was alone. He tiptoed across the floor and fell onto his bed. It took a long time for sleep to come. He heard his mother open his bedroom door and then close it again softly. He felt her lips brush his cheek. Only then did he feel a little safer. When he finally drifted off, he slept all that day and into the night, only getting up once to go to the bathroom. In the night he woke up three times, and each time he reached down beside his bed until he found his vodka, which he'd replaced with his sock-drawer stash. Eventually, he drank himself back to oblivion.

It was the sunlight streaming through his window, not his mom's call, that woke him up the next day. He sat up in bed and stretched. His clock read 11:15 a.m. That meant one of two things: either he needed to get some new batteries for his clock, or he'd slept for nearly twenty-one hours. He crawled out of bed and went into the bathroom, where he splashed cold water on his face and took an Aspirin—his head hurt: too much vodka and all, on an empty stomach.

Slowly the details of yesterday came back to him. He'd told Dad off, and nothing really terrible had happened. If he could, he would do it all over again. He grinned at his reflection in the mirror. "Let's get some breakfast," he said and headed downstairs.

Sixteen

The last thing Bryan expected to see when he got downstairs was his mom and Stella sitting together at the kitchen table, chatting in low voices over a pot of tea. They'd stopped doing that a long time ago. They looked up at him and smiled when he entered the room.

"Hi," he said, "What's going on?"

"Stella and I are catching up. Something we haven't done for a long time." Mom smiled at Stella. "Right?" Stella nodded back as if they were best friends. The tension between them, so evident since the accident, had vanished.

Bryan poured himself a big bowl of cereal and drowned it in milk. "Nobody woke me up, so don't bother getting mad at me," he defended himself. Mom just shrugged, as if it didn't matter that school had started over four hours ago. "Just sit down and eat your breakfast. I didn't call you, because I thought you needed to sleep."

"Okay," Bryan answered, puzzled, but relieved. "So, what's going on with you two?" It had been a long time since he'd seen them talking to each other like friends.

Stella reached across the table and put her hand on top of his mom's. "Go on, Izzy," she encouraged. "I'm here to back you up."

Uh-oh, here comes trouble.

"Thanks, Stella. Honey," she began, fixing her eyes on Bryan, "I was so upset about what happened last night, not just with you, but also with your dad...so I did what I should have done before things became...as bad as they have. I remembered I had a friend I could talk to, and I called Stella and asked her to come over and be with me, even though it's her day off."

"Nice," Bryan replied, his attention on the recipe on the back of the cereal box. "But what's this got to do with me?"

"Well, Stella and I had a long talk. I needed to run some things by her. So I've decided that, based on your behaviour, you haven't given me a lot of choice. I'm going to drive you to school and pick you up every day from now on, until things change."

"Mom, this is insane. I'm not ten years old anymore." Bryan couldn't believe his ears. Did she actually think this would make things better?

"Until you can be honest and tell me where you went the other night and what you did, I have to keep a close eye on you. Also, you're to check in every day with your school counsellor. Any more missed days and you are out."

"Aw, Mom."

"I mean it, Bryan, and Stella agrees with me. She wants to help, too. And stop scratching your stomach. You might want to change your shirt; something in that material might be irritating your skin. Anyway, the school has put you on contract. Either you show up—and show up ready to work—or there won't be any more chances for you. Mrs. Ward says you have being going to school so tired you can hardly keep your eyes open. She thinks you might be doing drugs. You're not, are you?" Her shoulders slumped, and for a moment, she seemed to lose her newfound confidence. "I haven't told any of this to your father. I haven't told him about the missing vodka, either." She bit her top lip. "I hate to think how he would react."

Before Mom could say another word, Bryan leaped in. "You know exactly how Dad would react. He'd kick my ass, he'd scream at me, and then he'd scream at you, and it would all be forgotten until the next time. Oh, and if he's really on a roll, he'll remind me of how much better Michelle was at life than I am. And then after that, the two of you would puzzle over why I wished I were dead."

"Bryan, please. Let me continue," she said very calmly. *She's sober*, Bryan speculated, studying her closely.

Stella added, "Quiet now, Bryan. It doesn't hurt to listen now and then." It had been a long time since Stella had asked anything of him. It surprised him so much he did what she asked, turning his attention back to his mother.

"Bryan, of course your father misses your sister, we all do, but he loves you, too."

"Don't give me that BS. We both know who Dad would choose to be alive if he could play god more than he already does . . . and it wouldn't be me."

Mom sighed. "I've set up another appointment with your psychiatrist," she said, not taking the bait. "You need to see her on a more regular basis."

"Set up all the appointments you like. I'm not going." Bryan stopped eating, glared at the two of them and stormed out of the kitchen, up the stairs and back into his room, slamming the door behind him. Only then did it occur to him that his father hadn't been present. Plus, she knew he'd been stealing her vodka. So, Stella knew about the booze, and she'd ratted him out.

Maybe that was the reason she'd cracked down on him so hard. She didn't want to share. Basically, she'd put him under house arrest, just because he had disappeared for a night. Ironic, wasn't it? They kept him in his room, so he would be 'safe,' and yet it was in his room where he did the most damage to himself. The whole weekend stretched out before him and he'd be stuck here. He groaned, but something in his mom's voice had made him realize that, for once, she meant what she said.

Shut away in his room, there wasn't much for Bryan to do but play guitar. He rummaged through his drawers, looking for an extra package of strings, but couldn't find one. Mustering his courage, he crept down the hall to Michelle's room and took one out of the spares she'd always kept in her dresser. He felt like a thief, but he needed to play, and besides, she didn't need them now. Back in his own room, he plugged his headphones into his amp so that the parents couldn't hear him, and he lost himself in the music. He knew he played better drunk than sober, and was thankful for the bottle of vodka hidden under his bed, thankful that Stella hadn't taken it. He'd have to figure out a new source now that Mom seemed to know everything. Maybe she'd be dumb enough not to lock up her own supply, but who cared. For now, he had enough to drink—and being drunk worked for him.

Mom kept her word, and Dad backed her up as much as he could. Bryan hadn't seen much of him since the morning of the big fight. But Mom drove him to school, picked him up after school (even if he didn't stay in school, he made sure to be back there at 3:30), and the rest of the time he spent in his room.

Michelle's apparition reappeared on a regular basis. Michelle the friendly ghost, returned to keep Little Bro company in his prison cell. Sometimes she smiled at Bryan, offered him advice on music. Other times she just sat very still and listened to him play, eyes closed, a slight smile on her lips. *What about my guitar?* she asked. *When are you going to check out my guitar?*

Shut up, man. You're dead. Bryan didn't mean it. He liked seeing Michelle, hearing her voice. Somewhere he had read that you are supposed to tell ghosts that they are dead, and so he did.

But Michelle understood about the cutting. She always had. It had been her idea in the first place. That didn't mean she got everything—*look what you left behind* . . .

In spite of not being allowed out, except to go school, Bryan had managed a few escapes out of the window in the dead of the night. He'd gone downtown to hang with Chris, staying away from the meth, sticking to pot—it creeped him out to see the effect of the drug on his new friend. He watched Chris watching him through paranoid eyes, listened as he ranted about all the people who were out to get him. Sometimes, when Chris talked, Bryan had to cover his nose or turn away, or he'd gag at the stench of his breath or the sight of his rotting teeth. He felt bad when he did that, as if it was some kind of a betrayal, but Chris didn't even notice.

They didn't get to hang together a lot, but Bryan tried to see him once a week when possible. And then one night, Chris wasn't smoking anymore. He'd started mainlining. "Smoking the shit doesn't do anything for me, man," he slurred. "Nothin' at all."

Bryan wouldn't have had the nerve to stick a needle in his arm, even if he wanted to. He didn't understand how Chris could do it, and he made his feelings clear. "I've done worse to myself," Chris told Bryan. They were walking down Granville Street. Bryan hadn't seen the person he had come to think of as his friend in over a week. He'd been writing exams, but they were over now and soon, grade twelve would be over, too.

In a few hours, the nightclubs would empty, and the street would fill up with drunk kids looking for fights and cops trying to stop them. "Wanna know my secret?" Chris offered. "Come on. I'll show you." He positioned himself under the faint light of a streetlamp. "You can see better here." He rolled up his sleeves and stuck out his arms. "I've been burning myself since I was a kid. Usually I burn, but I've cut, too." Most of the visible flesh on his arm had small, evenly sized scars in all stages of healing, some overlapping, and track marks, too. "I had a bad infection." Chris studied his arms as if he'd never seen them before. "Looks like I still have it." He wiped away a wad of pus, using his sleeve. "Anyway, I haven't done it for a while; a couple of days."

When Chris showed Bryan his hacked-up arms, Bryan wanted to tell him everything, but the words stuck in his throat. Instead, he put his arm around Chris's shoulders and blinked back unexpected tears. "Do you ever think of going home?" he asked.

"I don't have a home, unless you're talking about the hellhole I left." Chris picked at a pimple on his face, his eyes downcast. An awkward silence came between them. "Not an option," Chris added.

"Come on, man. Let's go get some food," Bryan said to fill in the empty space that now separated them. He unhooked his arm, astonished at the thinness of his friend. He'd felt like a skeleton—a thin layer of skin covered sharp, protruding bones— and Bryan thought Chris might break if he squeezed him, even a little bit.

"Yeah, food," Chris agreed weakly. "I could do with some food." His watery eyes lit up as much as they could at the mention of sustenance. And all the time they sat there in the greasy restaurant, under neon lights, Bryan thought about ways to tell Chris he had a secret, too, that he understood the appeal of the knife, but he couldn't do it. Something stopped him—the promise he'd made to himself after everything crashed: *I will never get close to anybody again for the rest of my life.* Up until now, that had been easy.

"You okay?" Chris stopped eating. "You look like someone just punched you in the gut."

"All good," Bryan lied, not meeting Chris's eyes. "But it's time for me to go." He stood awkwardly and threw a ten-dollar bill down on the table. "I'll see you later. Don't want to miss the last bus."

"The last bus," Chris repeated. "You should get on that bus and get out of here and never come back..." The sentence trailed off and he put down his hamburger, looking Bryan square in the eyes. "I mean it, man," he said. "You should get out of here and you should never return. You don't belong here. Nobody does." He rested his bony arms on the dirty table. From Bryan's vantage point, he looked like a little old man, not a kid in his teens.

Later, Bryan wished he had stayed, not walked out of there like the coward he'd become. But he didn't. Instead, he said "I'll see you soon," and left the diner as fast as he could. When he looked back, Chris was sitting motionless, eyes downcast, shoulders hunched, studying his burger and fries as if they were the only things that mattered in the world.

✕

Getting out of the house proved more and more difficult with Mom and Dad, and now Stella, watching his every move. Bryan knew he had to be very careful about sneaking out, but he felt bad about the way he'd left Chris, hungry and hurting, while he went home to a warm bed and people—annoying as they were— who cared about him.

So, a few days later, Bryan took a risk, skipped school and headed downtown armed with disinfectant and bandages. At first he couldn't find Chris in any of his regular haunts, and it scared the life out of him. Maybe he'd left it too long. He started asking some of the other street kids if they'd seen his friend. Some of them just gave him blank looks, most shrugged and walked away, but finally he found someone who thought they'd spotted Chris on a bench near the marina at the waterfront. After an exhaustive search (there were a lot of benches at the waterfront), Bryan found him, curled on a bench, a torn sleeping bag covering his slight body.

Bryan gently shook him awake. "Hey, dude. What are you doing?"

Chris sat up groggily. "What? I'm not bothering anyone. Oh, it's you." He took the sandwich Bryan offered him. "Tuna sandwich, a banana, cookies! Is it my birthday? Excellent, thanks."

"We're gonna fix up your arm, too," Bryan said awkwardly, pulling the disinfectant and bandages out of his pack before Chris could refuse his help. "It's grossing me out," he added by way of an explanation. He felt totally out of his element, but ready to argue with Chris if necessary.

But to Bryan's surprise Chris didn't offer up an argument, just held his arm out submissively. "It's killing me," he said. He winced when Bryan poured the disinfectant over the infected area and sat very still, munching on his sandwich until Bryan had bandaged it all up.

"Done," said Bryan, when he'd finished. "Now, I gotta get back to school. I'm already taking a big chance by skipping the morning."

"Smoke a joint first?"
"Sure."

"Thanks, Bryan." They sat on the bench smoking and looking at the boats in the marina. "I mean it. You are a true friend and I won't forget you."
"It's not a big deal."

CUT

That afternoon, Bryan couldn't concentrate in his English class. He missed the answers to two questions, and that made his English teacher's day. All the while, Chris's words kept spinning around in his head, and he wondered exactly what they meant: *I won't forget you.*

Seventeen

Sure enough, school called and told Stella he'd skipped, who told Mom, who totally lost it on him. "It was one class," Bryan protested, "and it was only Phys. Ed. This is totally not fair."

His objections fell on deaf ears. "Just when I thought I could trust you again, you skip school." His mom frowned at him from where she'd planted herself in his doorway. Her arms were crossed, and she had a look of determination on her face that Bryan had never seen before.

Perfect! Just what he needed right now.

Bryan had been startled when she'd knocked on his door; a few minutes earlier, and she would have caught him with the razor blade, and all hell would have broken loose. He squirmed uncomfortably. The slash on his stomach still hadn't healed, and he'd been examining it, poking at it with his fingers. Now it hurt even more.

"What are you doing up here, anyway?" he snapped. He'd been thinking about Chris, worrying, really.

"I was in Michelle's room. Stella suggested I think about cleaning it up, and I think maybe she's right. I just don't know if I can do it..." A small tear appeared in the corner of her eye. She dabbed at it with her fingertip. "I know it's silly, but if I clean out her room, it's like admitting that she's not coming back... and she's not, is she?"

Bryan watched her, never moving from his position on his bed. In the last couple of weeks, she'd changed, and he found her behaviour puzzling. For one thing, she'd cut down on her drinking, and for another, she didn't seem at all bothered by his dad's long absences from the house. In fact, she seemed to welcome them. She made the rules now, and she stuck with them, dumb as they were. And now this—talking to him about Michelle's room as if it were nothing.

"What's with you, lately? You're acting really weird. The only time you ever come up here is to nag me or go cry in Michelle's room," he added nastily, hoping she would leave, but she didn't, so he kept going. "Don't think I haven't noticed that Dad's never around and when he is, you guys don't talk." That didn't upset her either, so he tried another tactic. "Why can't you leave me alone? Go bug someone else."

Maybe you should give her a break. The Michelle Shrine, *as you call it, pisses me off, too.*

Take off, Michelle.

Mom blinked rapidly, but held her position. "I wish you'd agree to visit Dr. Spahic. It's been a couple of weeks or more," she said, ignoring everything he'd said to her.

"Okay. Done. But only if you lighten up a bit and leave me alone."

"Deal," she agreed. She pulled his door closed and then opened it again. "Oh, I forgot to tell you. Jessie called today."

"She did? What did she want?" He hated the hope he heard in his own voice.

"I thought you'd like to hear that. Anyway, I didn't ask her what she wanted. But she did ask that you call her back."

The door closed and her footsteps retreated down the stairs. He tried to digest this new piece of information. *Why had Jessie called?* He didn't have the time or the energy to think about her right now.

✕

His last meeting with Chris haunted him. Two weeks had passed since he'd fixed up that infected arm. He'd left with a sense of foreboding, and he hadn't returned. Because he had no way of contacting Chris, he knew he'd have to go and look for him, and that meant more trouble at home or at school. *That's why I haven't done it yet,* he lied to himself.

But last night he'd run out of excuses. After dinner, he climbed out of his bedroom window and hopped a bus downtown, determined to meet up with his friend. He'd thought it would be that easy, but it wasn't. He couldn't find him. Not anywhere. Chris had disappeared. *Poof!* Gone. Gone like he'd never existed. Bryan searched all of their old haunts; he combed the stinking back alleys off Granville Mall, where the addicts shot up and slept and sometimes died. No Chris. So then he went into the greasy diners, where you could hear rats if you stopped chewing and listened hard enough, but no Chris. He cruised the waterfront, checking each bench for his friend, but saw only people he'd never seen before. He asked everyone—cops, bums, hookers— "Have you seen my buddy, Chris? Tall dude, skinny with brown hair, three earrings in each ear, always wears a brown sweater and a leather jacket?"

The kids on the street said he'd gone back to Ontario, or up north to Prince George or east to Calgary, or overdosed, or had never existed. They looked at him blankly out of empty, pain-filled eyes. "Who's Chris?" they laughed.

At the very least he could have left Bryan a message—the streets looked after their own—one of the other kids would have let Bryan know, given him a reason . . . Bryan felt as if somebody had reached inside of him and ripped his heart out of his chest. That night, drunk in his room, he cut away the memory of his friend. He sliced him out of his flesh, but he had to cut deep and more than once to exorcise him.

Epitaph for One More Disappeared Person:

> *I have nothing to lose;*
> *I have nothing to fear.*
> *I'm just trying to disappear.*

He borrowed the lyrics from Nomeansno. He didn't think they'd care, either.

Not having Chris around made him think of Jessie. All the time, she loomed large in his head, but he hadn't called her back.

His interim report card reflected everything he thought about himself. For the first time in his school life, he earned not A's but C's and three of them. No surprise. He hadn't bothered to write two of his exams. He'd screwed up with Chris, just like he had with everyone else that mattered to him, so why not himself?

When Mom looked at his marks, she shook her head and handed the report card back to him without a word.

When Dad looked at his marks, he did exactly what Bryan knew he would do. He threw the report card on the floor, called Bryan a few choice names and stormed out of the room.

Cut.

Holy Parenting Skills, Mom and Dad. Great way to make me want to bring up my grades.

And when he told Dr. Spahic about their reactions, she'd raised her eyebrows and asked, "How did you feel about your marks? I mean, after all, that's all that really counts, isn't it?"

Eighteen

No matter how hard he tried to expel the image of Chris from his mind, he could still see him sitting on the bench at the waterfront, his arm bandaged, telling Bryan he'd never forget him. Why hadn't he seen it for what it was: *a goodbye.* He began to hit the downtown streets two or three times a week, mostly at night, to hunt for his friend, but no matter how hard he searched or how many people he talked to, he couldn't find him. Chris had disappeared off the streets, off the face of the earth, for all Bryan knew.

"Street kids come and they go. Your friend could be halfway across the country by now. After all, the weather's warmer in the east this time of year." That's what the cop he'd talked to tonight told him, and deep down, he knew it could be true. "Go home, kid—if you've got one. You're just going to get sick standing out here in the rain, or worse yet, mugged."

Bryan did as the cop advised. He walked all the way home and found himself standing on his front lawn, soaked to the bone. The rain dripped off his wet hair and trickled down the back of his shirt. They'd be cold downtown, those street kids whose names he had either never known or forgotten. He'd studied them closely tonight, just in case one of them happened to be Chris in disguise—that's how desperate he'd become.

Those kids stuck together in small groups, huddled beneath frayed awnings waiting for . . . what? The rain to stop? The world to get better? The past to undo? An unfamiliar emotion boiled in his stomach. He missed Chris—his one friend. His sudden disappearance made no sense. Like an idiot, he'd trusted Chris to stick around. Fool. People didn't matter. Nothing really mattered.

The houses on his street showed no signs of life, except for his: the TV pulsated a grey light that slid through gaps in the curtains. *Dad.* He'd taken to coming home late, after Bryan and his mom had eaten and gone to bed. His dad would go into the den, shut the door and watch TV, often falling asleep in his chair.

Bryan let himself in the back door. At first he didn't see her. She sat at the table, in the dim light, still as death, except for eyes that flickered in his direction when she spotted him. In front of her sat a half-empty bottle of vodka and a glass, its rim stained lipstick-pink.

They've had another fight. She's drunk. Stella shouldn't have left.

"Mom? Mom, what are you doing?" He flicked on the overhead light.

"Turn that off, please." She winced. "It hurts my eyes." He did as she asked without comment. He knew firsthand about bright lights and booze. "Thank you, Bryan. What am I doing here? I was worried about you. I wanted to know where you go when you leave without telling anyone. I know you sneak out at night. So I drove around looking for you, but I couldn't find you. I guess you didn't want to be found."

"No need to worry about me, Mom. I'm a big boy now. I'll be eighteen this summer."

"Eighteen this summer. Michelle would be almost twenty-two. She wasn't safe." She sniffled. "Give me a cigarette, please."

"Mom, you don't smoke. Mom, what's going on? Did you and Dad have another fight? The television is on. He's awake and sitting in the dark, as usual."

"He's watching TV. What a surprise." She laughed, a hollow laugh.

"Yeah, I didn't think he'd be out with you looking for me. Ha.

What a joke. I'm going to bed." *I feel sick.* Bryan pulled off his soggy jacket and put it on the back of a chair. It fell to the floor, where it stayed. He looked at his mother, at the lines on her face that he had never noticed before, and at her sad, dark eyes. He didn't need this right now. So much guilt. He thought the weight of the guilt might crush him. He thought the weight of his guilt equalled the weight of six feet of dirt pressing down on a narrow coffin.

"Ah . . ." Bryan searched for the magic words, the ones that would dispel the terrible sadness in her eyes, but he didn't have any, or there were none. Suddenly, the room spun, and he swayed and grasped the corner of the table to steady himself. *I feel terrible, but I can't leave her like this.* He waited for her—surely she would say something or do something besides stare off into space. Yet she sat silent and still, only her index finger moving, tracing tight circles on the tabletop.

Finally Bryan, afraid he might pass out in front of her, spoke. "I'm not feeling great, Mom. I'm going to head up to bed." She seemed to be in her own world. "Mom?"

She sighed and looked up at him, her eyes vacant and red-rimmed. Bryan waited. *Say something,* he prayed because he'd never seen her quite like this. In his belly, the knot of fear grew bigger, and the room spun faster. *Please be okay, Mom. Say something.*

"Goodnight, Bryan." A moan escaped her lips. "I guess I should say 'Sweet Dreams' or something motherly." Two tears bled out of the corners of her eyes, and more followed.

Bryan turned to leave, but stumbled and regained his balance. "Mom, I'm not well."

He remembered the time when he'd almost lifted up his shirt to show Jessie how he had shredded his own body, and how he had wanted to show Chris, but didn't. He couldn't, because what if they saw who he really was, and hated him? But maybe he'd got it all wrong. Maybe, if he revealed the truth, Mom would stop hating him, stop blaming him for Michelle's death because she would see how much he suffered, how much he hurt.

"Mom," he said, moving slowly around the table, until he stood directly in front of her. He swallowed the nausea rising in his throat. A bead of sweat rolled off his forehead into his eye. He really did feel sick, both boiling hot and freezing cold at the same time, but he had been feeling sick off and on for so long he'd learned to ignore it. He stumbled to the sink and splashed cold water on his face. Mom kept looking straight ahead as if he were invisible.

"Go to bed if you're not well." She dropped her eyes and when she spoke, he heard only disinterest in her voice. "I think I'll do the same myself. It's not much of a night, is it." Not a question, a statement. No answer expected.

Bryan didn't move. He wanted to, but his body wouldn't respond. Instead he leaned against the cool stainless-steel sink and waited, unsure if she'd finished speaking or not. Vegetable peelings from one more dinner that had not materialized littered the basin. "Mom, maybe we could talk."

The den door opened. "Isabelle! Who are you talking to in there? Is he home? I knew he'd be okay. I suppose you'll make him dinner. And if you do, I wouldn't mind some of the scraps." Mom winced at the sound of Dad's voice. Music blared from the TV.

Bryan rolled his eyes. "Can't he do anything for himself?"

"Perhaps we should talk," she agreed, ignoring Bryan's last comment.

The TV blared a jingle: *"Make housework fun, buy the Miracle Mop!"*

"For goodness sake! Close the door! I can't hear my own thoughts," she called out, her voice jagged.

The den door slammed shut.

Bryan moved slowly across the room and closed the kitchen door. He shuffled on leaden feet back to the table, pulled out a chair and sat down across from his mother. "Okay. Let's talk, Mom."

She spread her elbows across the tabletop and buried her head in her arms. He saw traces of grey in her hair that he didn't think had been there before. "Bryan," she said and he had to lean in close to hear her voice. "I don't think I can do this anymore." She lifted her head and sipped on her drink. "There. I said it. I'll say it again. I can't do this anymore."

What did she say?
Are you deaf? She said she's ditching you.

Go to hell, Michelle.
You heard her.

I said: Go. To. Hell.

I can't do this anymore. She said it so casually, almost as an after-thought. She'd written him off in five simple words?

I wanted to talk about me, not you! he wanted to scream at her. *I had stuff to tell you about me!* But he choked on the words.

After a long time he managed to speak. "Do *what* anymore?" Pretending he didn't already know. He struggled to sound brave. He faked it, like he had been taught to do. Like nothing meant something.

"All of this." She lifted her head and gestured around the room.

"You, your father, this house, this life. All of it. I just can't do it anymore."

The script he had written in his head didn't go like this. He had wanted to talk about himself, about what he was doing to himself. He wanted to be honest. He hadn't expected true confessions from his mother, from the one person he had counted on to be there for him. It wasn't fair. "Mom, I can't listen to this. I feel like I'm going to pass out."

The old mom, the one he knew, would have reacted to this. The mom he knew would have shown some worry, some concern. Instead this new one said, "Goodnight, Bryan," and sipped on her drink, concentrated on the glass as if it were a living thing.

His coat, with his smokes in the pocket, was on the floor. He grabbed it and stumbled up the stairs to his bathroom. As he passed Michelle's door, he gave it a hard kick.

All of this is your fault. Why'd you have to go and die? I hate you.

In the bathroom, he stripped off his clothes, turned on the shower and ducked under the stream of water. When the hot water hit the raw, open slashes on his stomach and arms, he bit down hard on his lip until it bled to stop himself from screaming. The pain embraced him, and he forced himself to move through it. *You are alive*, it confirmed. *You are real*. When he could, he studied the damage he had inflicted upon himself. The infected slash on his stomach had turned an angry red. He touched the raw, oozing red line, felt the puffiness beneath the scab and picked carefully at the inflamed crust on the surface until it broke away.

A stream of pus oozed out of the wound and disappeared down the drain. As the poison was released from his body, he heard the sound of someone sobbing. It took a moment before he realized the cries were coming from him.

His mother's words echoed in his mind: *I don't think I can do this anymore. All of this—you, your father, this house, this life.*

Well, join the club. Not coping seemed to be a Bianchi family trait. Except for Dad—the control freak. Dad, who'd only loved one of his kids—the one he couldn't see . . . not fair.

And so this is how it ends, Michelle. Are you happy now? What about you, Chris? Feeling good? He finished his shower, towelled off and took a handful of painkillers from the bottle in his bathroom cupboard. Not allowing himself the time to think about it, he swallowed them all.

Before he did anything else, he knew he needed to get in touch with Jessie. He owed her that. It took him a long time to compose the e-mail. He scheduled delivery of the e-mail to be postponed until late the next morning. While he wrote, he drank steadily from his bottle of vodka. When he had finished the e-mail, he didn't bother to re-read it; he just pressed SEND and then he picked up his guitar and held it gently in his lap. He waited to see if Michelle would come, but not even a dead chick showed any interest in being with him on this, his last night. He played a few songs quietly, but the music made him cry. He put the instrument down. The tomblike silence in the house told him that his parents had gone to bed. He looked at his watch. Not even midnight.

Will they preserve my room? Will they turn it into a shrine? Don't forget me when I'm gone.

Not likely.

He would be remembered as the bad guy, the black sheep, the straw that broke the camel's back, the aberration, the deviant, the loser . . . And he would take Michelle's secret to his grave.

If I die tonight, the only thing I will miss is my guitar.

Kurt Cobain: *I hate myself and want to die.*

Makes perfect sense. When people die, they disappear without a trace. They vanish.

I have nothing to lose; I have nothing to fear.
I'm just trying to disappear.

Finally, it would all stop.

Bryan took another handful of painkillers. He finished off the bottle. Then he finished off the vodka before he lay down under the covers and closed his eyes.

I am not scared.

Just vanishing myself.

Nineteen

What he missed:

Mom calling him and calling him, over and over again in the morning. Finally, annoyed and forcing her tired body up the stairs to his room. Knocking, softly at first and then more loudly. His still form under undisturbed covers sets off an alarm in her head. Then, she is flying down the stairs, sobbing. Trying to keep her hands from shaking so she can dial 911.

Later, there is Jessie's phone call, but nobody answers.

In the waiting area, Dad sits with his head in his hands. He is no longer in control.

In the emergency room, the ER doctor examines Bryan's mutilated body with gentle hands. She sends the empty bottle of painkillers to the lab. "What have you done?" she whispers and then she puts her emotions aside and does her job.

"I'll be there as soon as I can," Stella sobs when Isabelle calls her. She hangs up the phone and crosses herself. She knows Isabelle will not survive this twice. She packs her bags, because her vacation is over. Before she leaves, she looks up the number of the psychiatrist whom Bryan seems to trust.

Dr. Spahic is about to take Poppins to the vet when the phone rings. She thinks not to answer it. She will be even later than she is. But the caller hangs up and tries again, and again. "Hello," she says, trying not to sound irritated. She listens to the caller's distraught message. "Thank you," she says. She puts Poppins down and plants a kiss on her nose. "We will have to go to the vet another day." She leaves the house in her slippers. Only later does she realize how silly she looks.

In another hospital, on the edge of downtown, Chris is discharged from Emergency. His throat is raw from the stomach tube, and he shakes. Withdrawal terrifies him. Even though he is very afraid of failure, he agrees to go to detox. He agrees because he has a friend now—Bryan—and that might make life worth living.

Michelle hovers over the emergency room cot. She doesn't know if he can hear her anymore. *Please don't die. I will leave you alone if you don't die,* she promises even though she is petrified of being without her family.

✕

It is bedtime. In his dream. If that is what this hellhole is. He looks at his hands. They are small and chubby; there is dirt under his fingernails. He remembers now; they planted carrots today. Bryan kneels beside big-sister Michelle. They say their nighttime prayer together. They do not giggle even though they think it is funny. They do not giggle because even though Daddy does not believe in God, he thinks it is important that his children are educated in the Christian faith. Daddy stands in the doorway and watches them. Daddy is always watching them.

> *Now I lay me down to sleep,*
> *I pray the Lord my soul to keep.*
> *If I should die before I wake,*
> *I pray the Lord my soul to take.*

"I think he's waking up. Bryan? Bryan? Can you hear me? You are in the hospital. My name is Dr. Chung."

Sick. Cold. But the hand on my forehead is soothing.

"Give him two CCs of this to calm him down and keep a close eye on him. Call me if there are any changes, otherwise I'll check back in about twenty minutes."

Cold liquid moving through my veins. Dark here.

"Fight, Bryan." It is the same soft-spoken female as before. It is the voice that belongs to the hand.

What's happening to me? Where am I? Everything hurts. Lips so dry. Whose voices are those? The soles of my feet are burning. Hot. Need water. Blood. So much blood—on the road, on the windshield, on my hands. Is it mine? So sticky and hot. Somebody is crying. Not Michelle. Not Michelle!

"Hello, Bryan. If you can hear me, please try to be calm."

A different voice from the other place, the place I tried to leave. So where am I? I know that voice.

Shit, Bry. Can't you hear me or see me?

Michelle.

Yeah. It's me. Go home, Bryan. Please.

Bryan's body fights the restraints. Beneath his eyelids his eyes roll back and forth. There is an IV in his left arm, and a tube runs down his esophagus to his stomach. He is hooked up to a heart monitor that beeps irregularly. His face is pale grey, and all colour has drained from his lips. Two doctors and three nurses stand over him, while a fourth applies medicine to his slashes.

"His EKG is improving, but we're not there yet." Dr. Chung is the emergency room doctor, the one who speaks to him so gently and touches him so softly.

The other physician is Dr. Spahic. "Are his toxicity tests back yet?" she asks one of the nurses.

He hands her a form. "They found traces of alcohol, Zeldox, and lots of Codeine."

"Mmm, he's only been on the Zeldox for a month. I started him on a very low dose. I don't like to put kids on anti-depressants unless it's absolutely necessary. The alcohol, and the codeine mixed with the Zeldox could have brought on the psychotic episode. No other drugs showed up?"

"A residual amount of THC."

"Hmm." Dr. Spahic's voice is distressed. "How could I have missed the fact that he self-injures?"

"It's easy. They hide it. I've seen enough to know that. If he hadn't overdosed, he'd have ended up here anyway. Some of his wounds are septic."

"Oh, my God. Who found him?"
"His mother. She's in the waiting room with her husband. She's pretty shaken."

"They lost their daughter almost two years ago. Did she tell you what happened?"

"I gather she and Bryan had argued the night before. He went to bed upset and when she went to wake him up for school . . . well, you can guess the rest . . ."

"Did anyone find a note?"
"Not yet."

Bryan mumbles more unintelligible words and phrases. The doctors confer together and inject another dose of tranquilizer into his IV. Soon he is quiet.

He drifts back down the narrow dark tunnel into blackness, into the relentless dream that has haunted him for nearly two years. The dream that always returns, as soon as he is sober, no matter what he does.

Twenty

The dream always opens in the real world, catapulting Bryan into the night Michelle died. He is both director and actor, hovering between the two roles, walking a tightrope that spans truth and imagination. Because there is no escape, the dream quickly morphs into a nightmare.

In the dream, as in real life, Michelle had found herself at the house party, against her will. She'd been sent to pick him up— Dad and Mom only agreed to extend his curfew if he agreed to a ride home. Michelle had been pissed, but Bryan begged her, and, in the end, she conceded. She'd never been one for parties, for small talk, but here she was and once she'd had a few beers, she started to enjoy herself. There were a few kids from school, mixed in with strange faces, and then someone brought out the guitars, and Michelle relaxed.

Bryan had looked forward to the party. He'd go anywhere, if it meant he'd be with Jessie. And then they had that stupid fight. His fault. All the horrible accusations he'd thrown at her were repeated in the nightmare. Bryan wanted to leave. He wanted to get her out of there and take back all those hurtful words. "Go," Jessie taunted. "Grow up, or leave. It's your choice." She disappeared into the crowd.

He grabbed his coat. "Come on, Michelle, let's get out of here." But Michelle wasn't ready to leave. "Chill, Bryan. Have another beer or something." Someone made a crack about her babysitting her little brother. She laughed at him, like they all did. No, Michelle wasn't going anywhere. She had everything she ever needed: a guitar in her hand, a cigarette in her mouth, and a beer at her feet. Mom and Dad would kill her for drinking when she had the car. Bryan would turn sixteen in a week and then he'd have his driver's license, too. He'd be free.

He watched out of the corner of his eye as Michelle opened another beer and then took a hit of the joint circling the room. God, would they ever leave? Outside, the rain pounded down, but inside, the swell of bodies created a furnace-like atmosphere. Bryan went to the kitchen and poured himself a big glass of vodka. He added a bit of orange juice. "Chug," someone encouraged and others joined in. "Chug." It went down easily, more so than he'd expected. Someone slapped him on the back. "Way to go." And then he had a beer in his hand and a lot of friends. The room spun, but he took a few deep breaths, and it stopped.

In the nightmare, real life and dream life got all mixed up. Whose idea had it finally been to leave in the end? He couldn't remember, but he did know that it had been his idea to drive. Maybe if they'd left before . . . before what? Another beer, another toke? Would it have made any difference at all? Jessie left before him— alone, but she left him there.

"Damn. Michelle. Let's go."

"Sure, Bry. Soon." But it didn't matter what he wanted. Once Michelle picked up a guitar, time meant nothing to her. Bryan studied his sister. He hated her right now. Hated her because she played guitar better, made friends faster, and refused to listen to him. Look at her, surrounded by adoring fans . . . She wore her trademark long-sleeved, button-up shirt and faded, ripped, jeans. Just like he did. *Why don't you ever wear a short-sleeved shirt, sister?* Only Bryan knew the answer—Michelle's bloody secret—he'd discovered it by accident one day when he'd barged into her room.

Zig-zag cuts. Arms and legs and stomach. Blood. Panicked eyes. "Don't tell them. Promise me you won't tell them."

"But why?"
"They wouldn't understand."
"No, but why are you doing it?"
"Because I can feel. Because I bleed like everyone else. I can feel something. I don't know how to explain it. I can't stop."

"Mom will find out."

"She hasn't yet. She's got other things on her mind, bigger problems."

"Like what?"

"Like Dad."

Bryan is scared. Nobody tells him anything. "What's wrong with Dad? Is Dad sick?"

"Jesus, Bryan. You don't know anything about what goes on in this family. You're such a baby. Mom might not say much, but if you watched her eyes, you'd know."

Michelle's words are slurred—she speaks in slow motion and can't seem to pronounce anything right. This in-his-dream Michelle stands in front of him and holds a razor blade stained crimson. She is a stranger to him. This Michelle has mean little eyes that look right through him. "It's in my guitar, isn't it, Little Bro? The missing piece. Why don't you look for it?"

Suddenly reality disintegrates.

This Michelle throws back her head and laughs out loud. Her teeth are elongated and sharp, like a vampire's. What have you done to my sister? This Michelle holds up the razor blade, waves it in Bryan's face. "Go ahead, try it. You might like it. You'd be surprised at how good it feels."

This Michelle rushes at Bryan and tackles him to the ground, shrieking maniacally. "Your turn, Little Bro." And the singing begins again, a familiar tune, a song he likes: Nirvana's "Blandest."

Bryan tries to raise his hands to protect his face, but he can't move them. Michelle begins to slash and bite. Bryan feels the cold steel cutting into his cheek, branding his forehead, piercing his nose. Michelle's fangs puncture the soft skin over his jugular vein. Blood flows out of his eyes, blinding him.

Make it go away. Go away.

Darkness. Light. Life. Death.

"Do you really think you killed me, Bryan?"

I'm sorry. I'm so sorry.

Twenty-one

Bryan's parents sat quietly across from each other in the austere waiting room. Each lost in thought, in recriminations. They'd been told Dr. Spahic would speak to them after she'd seen Bryan and conferred with the ER doctor. They anticipated her arrival in their own way. Each in their own private hell. Although the words remained unspoken, they blamed each other.

They exchanged as few words as possible. Bryan's mother avoided her husband's cold accusing eyes. Instead, she unconsciously picked at her cuticles while staring intently at the embroidered words on the sign tacked on the wall opposite her. It read:

> *God moves in a mysterious way,*
> *His wonders to perform.*
> *He plants His footsteps in the sea,*
> *And rides upon the storm.*

If the words were meant to provide comfort, they had the opposite effect on her. God's mysterious ways were no excuse for the cruelty he had rained upon her over the past two years.

The Bianchis had positioned themselves in the waiting room like opposing forces on the battlefield of life. It wouldn't take much for either one to launch an attack. Both remembered another time, another waiting room. Another child.

"We are so sorry..." Those words forever burned in both of their memories. They wear the scars of those words in the deep crevasses in their foreheads and the heavy black circles under their eyes. But there are scars that can't be seen on their faces—a broken marriage, a destroyed family.

Michelle had been a good girl. They agreed on nothing else, but they agreed on this.

Bryan is a good boy, too. He is their only boy.

His mother started to cry again, but his father made no move to comfort her. He knew there was nothing he could offer her that she would accept. The ER doctor—Dr. Chung, he thought her name was—seemed competent enough, but the things she'd said about Bryan shocked him. She blamed his suicide attempt on something she called a psychotic episode. "Think of it as a break from reality," she explained. "The patient becomes confused about where he is, about what is real and what isn't. Often he or she will hear voices." Her clinical tone switched to one of compassion. "I understand from his psychiatrist, Dr. Spahic, that your daughter passed away in an accident almost two years ago. It seems that your son has been . . . not only hearing her voice, but also seeing her. He feels guilt about her death. And . . . well, he feels that he can't compete with her memory."

She waited a moment for this to sink in before continuing. "I'm not sure if you are aware of this, but your son has been hurting himself. We call it self-mutilation."

Bryan's mother whimpered and covered her eyes. "Oh, my God," she sobbed.

Dr. Chung patted her on the shoulder. "I realize how hard this must be for you," she sympathized.

"Please continue," snapped Bryan's father. Dr. Chung knew everyone reacted to these situations differently, but she couldn't help but dislike this cold man.

"As you know, his psychiatrist had just started him on an antidepressant, Zeldox, and that mixed with alcohol is very dangerous. We are doing our best to help him . . . some of his cuts are septic. He's got a long road ahead of him. I'll keep you apprised of the situation."

As soon as she'd left the room, Bryan's father exploded. "How the hell could all of this have been going on beneath our noses, and neither of us noticed? You're with him every day, Isabelle. Are you blind, or just too drunk most of the time to see what was going on?"

"Not now," his wife pleaded. "Please, not now . . ."

"Ahem. Excuse me. If I could just have a word?" Dr. Spahic stood at the door to the waiting room. She'd been there long enough to understand why Bryan's behaviour had deteriorated so much in the last month. *Poor kid*, she thought. *Parents sure know how to screw things up.*

"Dr. Spahic!" Bryan's mother leaped up from her chair and ran to her. "Please tell me Bryan is going to be okay! I can't do this again . . ." She collapsed in Dr. Spahic's comforting arms.

Dr. Spahic led her back to her chair and helped her to sit down. She took out a Kleenex. "Here you are," she said softly. "Take a nice deep breath and then we can talk." Out of the corner of her eye, she saw Bryan's father's jaw set. "Dr. Bianchi, let's just give your wife a minute. This is very difficult for her . . . and for you, too."

"Are you aware, doctor, that you are wearing pink slippers?" Before she could reply, he added, "Not very professional, which doesn't surprise me in the least. A professional would have seen this coming and done something about it."

She eyed him coldly, biting back her response. "Nice to meet you, at last, Dr. Bianchi. I wanted to go over the notes from Dr. Chung, who admitted Bryan." She opened the file she'd brought in with her, but Bryan's mother interrupted her.

"Can I please see my son?"

Dr. Spahic's heart went out to her. "Is there anyone else you'd like to be here with you?"

"Stella . . . Bryan's nanny . . . our housekeeper . . . will be here as soon as she can."

"I know who Stella is," replied Dr. Spahic. "Bryan thinks very highly of her."

"I demand to see him!" Bryan's father shouted. "And after that, I'd like a word with you about your treatment, or should I say *mis*treatment."

"I'm sorry, but as I was about to explain to Bryan's mother, this is neither advisable nor possible at the moment. Bryan's heavily drugged because he is extremely agitated. He is in restraints and unaware of his environment."

"In restraints? He's tied up. Oh, God." The little colour she had left drained out of Bryan's mother's face, and she folded into herself.

Dr. Spahic saw that Mrs. Bianchi's husband did not reach out, did not touch her, only glared at her disdainfully. "For God's sake, Isabelle! If you control yourself, we might get some answers." He dismissed her with the wave of a hand. "I apologize for my wife. Now go on, doctor. Why is he in restraints?"

"We are doing everything we can to ensure that Bryan won't hurt himself."

"As I said earlier, you should have seen this coming, Dr. Spahic. What do I pay you for?"

"Dr. Bianchi, I might have seen it coming, if I had been seeing Bryan on a regular basis, but I've only been seeing him off and on for the last two months."

"Why didn't anyone tell me this? Why didn't you tell me this?" He shot a look of malice at his wife.

"I wanted to," she said, "but you get so angry."

"Well, I wonder why that would be?" he sneered. "Well, congratulations. Your babying him has landed him in the loony bin."

"Please," Dr. Spahic interjected, fighting not to lose control with this arrogant man. "This would be a lot easier if you'd stop—" she'd been about to say "bullying your wife," but caught herself in time. "...If you'd just listen to what I have to tell you."

"Someone has to accept the blame," said Bryan's father under his breath.

Dr. Spahic ignored him. She sat down and waited for him to follow suit. "The most important thing we can do for Bryan right now is, as I've already said, to calm him down. I'd advise you both to go home and get some rest. I'll let you know as soon as you can see him."

"Will he survive?" Bryan's mother interjected.

"Yes. Although his mental state will depend a lot on you two. That said, I'd like to set up an appointment for both of you to meet with me tomorrow. Either separately or together," she added.

"I don't understand what the other doctor said. Why would Bryan hurt himself? Why would he do that?" Bryan's mother wrung her hands together.

"It's a good question, Mrs. Bianchi. People who self-injure often cut, or burn themselves, in order to feel better. I know it sounds

like a contradiction, but if you understand the physiology behind it, it's actually quite logical."

"It's logical to take a knife to yourself? What kind of a quack are
you?"

"Please, Dr. Bianchi. If you would just let me explain: when
Bryan is unable to cope with a stressful situation—or when he
can't figure out where he ends and others begin—he becomes
overwhelmed by self-hatred. He turns his anger inward and by
cutting, he releases some of the pressure he feels. When he cuts,
endorphins are released, just like when we exercise, for example.
The endorphins cause him to feel better temporarily, and so he
cuts again. It can become an addictive behaviour. Some might
even call it self-preservation rather than self-destruction."

"What a bunch of bull-crap. I'm certainly not interested in your
psychobabble. And I've no interest in a meeting with you. I hold
you accountable for all of this." Bryan's father rose angrily. "Let's
go, Isabelle. My wife and I will discuss this in the car. Please call
us if there are any changes through the night."

"Mrs. Bianchi, would you be willing to talk to me?" Dr. Spahic
said softly. She placed a gentle hand on Bryan's mother's shoulder. "It might be very important to Bryan's recovery."

Bryan's mother nodded. "Yes. Of course. Anything."

"Fine. Actually, why don't we say noon tomorrow?"

"Of course. And thank you."

"Come on, Isabelle."

Bryan's mother followed her husband out of the waiting room and down the long corridor. She kept a good five paces behind him, out of fear, or perhaps loathing, Dr. Spahic speculated. Bryan hadn't exaggerated when he'd described his father. "It's no wonder some kids just can't cope," she said to herself sadly.

Before leaving the hospital, Dr. Spahic checked in on Bryan. He'd settled slightly, so the tranquilizers had begun to kick in. Still he tossed and turned in his sleep, eyes fluttering, muttering unintelligible words and phrases. She studied his charts and left instructions that, with Dr. Chung's approval, he should remain in restraints until she saw him in the morning. She re-checked the bandages that covered most of his torso and arms. The infection worried her. She'd seen it all before, but that didn't make it any easier.

She put her hand on Bryan's hot forehead. "You're safe now."

Twenty-two

"I don't want to see them. Especially him. They won't understand." Bryan glared at Dr. Spahic.

She held his gaze. "You don't have to see anyone until you feel that you are ready." She smiled. "Except me, of course, the other patients, and the nursing staff." She handed him two cards. "Stella wanted you to have this, and the other one is from your mom."

"Thanks." He grinned. "I can handle cards. Look, I'm feeling okay now. It was a stupid thing that I did. I'm still alive and I'm ready to get out of here."

"Your wounds haven't healed, and you still have an infection, so you're not leaving yet."

It had been four days since Bryan had been admitted to Emergency. Once his doctors had judged him fully out of danger, they moved him to the Psychiatric Ward for observation.

His nightmares had subsided, but real sleep continued to elude him. He saw Dr. Spahic every morning, and although she questioned him gently, she didn't push him any further than he felt willing to go.

This morning, when he asked, she'd explained his course of treatment to him. "Do you remember what you did?"

"I don't want to think about it right now." Bryan closed his eyes to shut out the world. "I took some pills, had a bit to drink. I'm okay now. I want to go home."

"You're still considered a Level-Four patient, and therefore you are not free to leave here. There's no negotiating on this point."

"Level Four? What does that mean? That I'm going to kill myself as soon as I have the chance?"

"Well, will you?"

"I don't know. It's nobody's business anyway. Maybe I will, unless you all back off. It's not like the parents paid any attention before, so why all the concern?" *It's not like I'll be missed*, he thought, lying back and closing his eyes. "I'm really tired."

"That's a typical reaction to the medication. Over the next few days, I'll reduce the dosage of the tranquilizer and reintroduce the anti-psychotic into your system," Dr. Spahic explained. "You and I will begin an active course of therapy at the end of the week if all goes as it should. Meaning you will stay here. We will meet every day for an hour—you know the routine—and we will continue to do that until you feel confident in yourself . . . more able to cope."

"Don't hold your breath," protested Bryan. "What makes you so sure I've ever figured out how to cope? I think I just hid it better. I know what's wrong with me. I'm depressed, okay? I hate peo-ple. I hate myself. Give me one reason not to? Besides, a person can't feel good all the time. Not even a normal one."

"True," agreed Dr. Spahic. "Pretending doesn't work."

"Not according to my dad."

"Your dad isn't always right."

News to me. Did she mean it?

He continued to be surprised each time Dr. Spahic agreed with him. For so long, people—his teachers, his shrinks, his parents, everyone—had demanded that he get a grip, that he move on, that he get over it, and here she was telling him that it was okay to feel the way he did. He wanted so badly to trust her. She told the truth, and in that way, she reminded him of Jessie, and thinking of Jessie made him feel sad. He remembered that he had sent her an e-mail the night he'd overdosed. He only remembered bits and pieces of what he'd said.

Confusion. Fog.

He told Dr. Spahic about his nightmares. She didn't get angry with him for not mentioning them before, like he'd thought she would. Instead, she suggested that he record his dreams. She even provided him with a laptop to make it easier. "Give it a try," she recommended, when he protested. "You're a musician, aren't you? You write songs. It's almost the same thing, except the words are all about you." Nobody had ever referred to him as a musician before, and even though he didn't show it, he felt pleased.

Pencils and pens were not allowed on the ward, for obvious reasons. "But I guess I can't cut myself with a laptop," he joked. "I'll give it a shot, if you think it will help."

So far Bryan had only managed to input the day and date followed by his name. Below his name, he typed, *I promise I won't tell*, over and over again. He refused to show Dr. Spahic what he'd written.

Over the next few days, the hospital routine became Bryan's routine. He even got used to the food. He didn't like it, he'd have preferred his mom's cooking, but as his cuts healed and the fever subsided, his appetite returned. Being classified high-risk meant no metal cutlery, no belts, no shoes, and especially no razors—a nurse shaved his face once a week. There were lots of things he didn't like about being there, and he listed them in a Word document. He hated the hospital robes and slippers they made him wear. Heavy metal doors barred anyone from entering or leaving the psych ward unless they knew the lock codes. All day, Bryan listened to the cries, or the crazy laughter, or the rantings of his fellow prisoners. The ward quieted down at night, but not much. Everyone, except the most robotic, wanted to escape. Getting out was the main topic of conversation in the common room.

Jail must be like this, he thought.

After a week, and at Dr. Spahic's encouragement, Bryan ventured out of his room and wandered down the hall to the communal games room. A handful of patients stared at the TV. Just like Dad. He made no effort to communicate with them and carefully avoided eye contact. *I might be suicidal, but the rest of them are clearly crazy.*

He only hung around long enough to realize he didn't belong there. *Get used to it*, he scolded himself. He returned to his sterile room, where he pulled his chair over to the window, rested his elbows on the sill and stared out into the bleak, cloudy day. There was no escape. Black, metal bars turned the dreary view into fractured picture frames. Six separate rectangles—three on the top and three on the bottom. Each offered a unique vista of the outside. In two of the upper frames he could see only clouds, or sky, but the third one showed the trees that surrounded the hospital grounds, and beyond them, the highway. The lower frames highlighted the cars in the parking lot and the grey, squat buildings beyond the flowerbeds. He counted the passing days, and then weeks, by the steadily lengthening days that hinted of summer. Bryan spent hours staring out the window, longing for the outside, but half-convinced he couldn't survive out there. Knowing, also, that he deserved to be locked up.

He refused to see anyone, but he knew they wanted to see him— Mom, Dad, Stella, Jessie and even her parents, had requested visits. He didn't see Jessie, but he thought about her a lot. He regretted how he'd treated her, and he put it all down in his laptop.

In spite of his determination not to mingle with the other patients, he couldn't isolate himself in his room all day and all night. Slowly, he got to know some of them. There were three other cutters, or self-abusers, as Dr. Spahic preferred to call them, on the ward. Shelley picked at her face and pulled out her hair by the handful, and Bryan stayed out of her way. Derek banged his head against any hard surface he could find and refused to speak, and Lisa, who had burn marks covering nearly every inch of her body, always greeted Bryan with a wide smile. Of all of them, he thought maybe Lisa might be worth getting to know.

Some of the other kids were in for straight substance abuse or eating disorders and others because they had been rescued during suicide attempts. As far as he could tell, all of them had only two things in common: 1. They all thought Dr. Spahic was pretty cool. 2. None of them belonged outside. And so, those who were able, including Bryan, took advantage of the online classes offered. Soon he discovered he actually preferred distance learning, away from the mocking stares and the stupid remarks. He worked hard, at his own pace, and achieved excellent marks.

His days varied little. At 7:30, breakfast arrived in his room. At 8:00, an orderly brought him his meds and stood by to make sure he swallowed them. Then the kindly nurse whose voice he recalled from his first night took his vital signs, and scrutinized his body for new wounds. She needn't have worried. Bryan had made no attempt to hurt himself, although he bit his nails until the skin around them bled. He met Dr. Spahic at 11:30 for an hour, followed by lunch, school and an optional afternoon group therapy session, which he'd considered attending, but hadn't yet.

Dr. Spahic insisted on a barrage of tests, most of them endured under the stare of other shrinks. He took them reluctantly, and shaped his answers according to what he thought she wanted to hear.

One morning, when he entered her office, Dr. Spahic was not her usual agreeable self. She looked at him and frowned. As soon as he settled, she spoke. "Bryan, you have been wasting my time and yours."

"Well, I know I've been wasting mine," he replied.
"I'm very serious about this," she said.
"So am I."
"I know you are manipulating your test results. You're not being honest. I can't help you if you don't cooperate. So, from now on we just talk. No more tests."
"Whatever. I never wanted to do the dumb tests anyway."

"I know. My mistake. I should have listened to you." She dug around in her purse. "I brought you a photo of Poppins and Kody, but I can't find it. Maybe I left it at home . . . anyway, next time . . . but I'm sorry I didn't listen. You were right." There, she'd done it again—agreed with him.

"Thanks," he muttered. "Oh, and you gave me the photo yesterday." He laughed and she joined in.

"Your mom wants to know if you'd like your guitar?"

"Aren't they worried I might garrote myself? Kidding. Tell her yes."

"Great. Next. I understand your nightmares were quite severe last night?"

This question caught Bryan off guard. Dr. Spahic saw his puzzlement. "You were screaming in your sleep. Not the first time, but the most-distressed."

"I'd rather not talk about it."

"I'm sure you've heard that dreams are sometimes the window to our soul," said Dr. Spahic. "They are a way for your subconscious to work out your problems and stresses. Have you been keeping your computer journal and recording your dreams and thoughts as I suggested?"

Bryan picked at the loose material on the arm of the chair. His leg bounced up and down. She was always on him about the so-called 'dream diaries.'

"Okay, I'm writing stuff, but it's kind of personal." In truth, he loved the writing and poured all of his thoughts into the computer. Sometimes he wrote for two hours or more, but he made sure to always delete his words before he, or anyone else, could read them.

Dr. Spahic gave him the thumbs-up. "I'm thrilled that you are writing. I'm thrilled you enjoy it. But the key question is: are you finding it helpful?"

"I don't know. I guess it is."

"Is it helping you to remember?"

"I don't want to remember!" Bryan shouted. He began to shake. "Don't you get it? I don't want to remember. 'Move on. Get on with your life.' That's what he said. 'You can't go back in time. You're going to have to learn to live with what you did.' And then he said. 'I wish it had been you . . . ' Well, that's what I'm doing now—learning to live with myself."

"Who said that, Bryan? Who said that to you?" Dr. Spahic spoke softly, as if he were a small child. "They were wrong. None of those things are true."

"My father." Bryan leaped from his chair, tears streaming down his face. "Who else? The only person besides me who knows what I did. My father." He couldn't stay in there a second longer. He felt bile in his throat. "I'm sorry." He turned and ran from her office, not stopping until he reached his own room, where he threw himself onto his bed and covered his head with his pillow.

And that's where he stayed for the rest of the day. He didn't eat the meatloaf at dinner, and the medical team left him alone, merely checking on him as required. When he began to scratch and tear at the scars on his stomach and arms, the nurse administered a shot in his arm that sent him into a drugged sleep.

He saw Michelle in his dream. She sat by him and rubbed his head. "It's okay, Bry," she whispered. "It's not your fault."

Twenty-three

His guitar, the knock-off Fender that his mother had delivered two days ago, lay on the green vinyl chair that sat at the end of Bryan's hospital bed. Having bequeathed it to Jessie in his hasty last e-mail, he hadn't expected to ever see it again. But of course, he was still here, and so was his guitar. He had wanted her to have it, but he had wanted to be dead, and that hadn't turned out either. He'd joked with Dr. Spahic when she'd okayed the guitar, but if he'd really wanted to, he could turn it into a lethal weapon. He knew her permission to keep it in his room translated into a vote of confidence. He was surprised how much that meant to him.

He'd found a short note from Mom taped onto the neck of the guitar. It read simply: *I miss you, but I understand you need time. Love, Mom.* He put it in the drawer beside his bed. Even though he knew exactly what it said, he reread it often. "I'm starting to think I'd like to see my mom soon," he told Dr. Spahic in their next session.

"Whenever you're ready," she nodded, but smiled, unable to hide her pleasure.

The hospital was a noisy place, but particularly in the mornings. Bryan often woke early and lay in bed listening to the sounds of the orderlies, nurses and doctors as they moved up and down the hallway. Sometimes he drifted back to sleep, or slipped out of bed to sit by the window and watch the outside world come to life. Now that he had his guitar, he had a purpose. He'd wake up, tiptoe out of bed and shut his door. Then he'd drag his chair over to the window and spend the time he had before breakfast playing softly. At first he'd been hesitant—afraid that he'd lost the ability to play, just as he'd lost the capacity to go on living, but the guitar felt like an old friend in his hands, and the notes came easily.

Slowly, it became his constant companion. When he wasn't doing schoolwork, or in therapy, he wrote in his laptop, often turning his thoughts into songs. Slowly, a little bit each day, he felt his depression lifting. His nightmares became less frequent and more meaningful. Last night he'd dreamt about a guitar—not his, but Michelle's Rosa Hurricane. In the morning he'd gone straight to his computer and typed: *The guitar holds something for me. An answer, but to what question? What does it have to tell me?*

Bryan had been back on his anti-depressants for a week, not Zeldox, but a drug that agreed with his system. For the first time since he'd been hospitalized, he felt both hungry and curious about events outside of his room. To his surprise, he wolfed down the overcooked eggs and cold, soggy toast, eating every last crumb on his plate. For the first time since he had been admitted, he got dressed, putting on jeans and a T-shirt, then made his way to the common room at the end of the hall. He'd expected to find it empty at this hour of the day, and he wasn't disappointed. He turned on the TV and surfed the channels, absentmindedly, not surprised to find nothing on of interest. He wandered over to the bulletin board and scanned through the day's activities. Beside the usual pottery, drawing and cards classes, he spotted a group therapy meeting scheduled for 10:00 a.m., led by Dr. Spahic. Why not? For weeks, she'd encouraged him to check it out. *I'll go*, he decided. *If it's really lame, I'll leave.*

He showed up fifteen minutes earlier than the other kids. He'd planned it that way so that he wouldn't have to deal with a group of strangers staring at him when he entered the room. He didn't want to draw any attention to himself, so he chose a chair at the edge of the room and watched the other kids appear one by one or in small groups of two or three. Most of them ignored him, although a couple nodded at him tentatively. Bryan sat back in his chair, thumbs in his pocket, eyes narrowed, exuding a confidence he did not feel at all. The friendly kids got a curt nod for their efforts, the rest he looked right through.

His hard demeanor belied both the butterflies in his stomach and the pounding in his chest. His every move suggested 'fuck you.'

Dr. Spahic arrived five minutes after the last kid sat down. "Sorry I'm late," she apologized. "No excuse, just not organized today." She smiled at no one in particular and sat down, then stood up again to remove her coat. "Cat hairs," she muttered. "but I suppose you're all used to that by now." She sighed and threw her coat in the general direction of her chair. It missed and hit the floor, but she didn't seem to notice. Bryan smiled on the inside, but he remained stone-faced.

She scanned the room, but she did not single Bryan out. He thanked her silently for understanding the supreme effort it took for him to be there.

"Okay. Pull your chairs into a circle," she instructed, "I think today we'll begin with introductions. You know, just say your name and that's it."

"That's retarded. We all know each other—well, not him—the cutter." The speaker scowled at Bryan, and Bryan scowled back at him. *Asshole.*

"Shut up, Dylan. You'll get kicked out if you call people names," one of the girls said. Everyone else remained silent. A handful of them squirmed. Except for the girl who had risen to his defense, they all seemed to fear the tall, scowling kid. Bryan slyly summed up his adversary. A bully. He was tall, skinny, blonde-haired, a few years younger, watery-eyed and covered in pimples. The kid, Dylan, pulled his baseball cap down over his eyes and slouched deeper into his chair, but not before he turned to the girl and drew his hand across his throat.

"Thank you for that, Dylan," said Dr. Spahic. Clearly she'd missed the threatening gesture. "But you know the rules. We just talk about ourselves, not others in the group." She winked at Bryan. "This is Dylan," she said. "Who's next?"

"I'm Sara." It was the girl who'd told Dylan to shut up. "Dylan's an idiot. Sorry, Dr. Spahic—I forgot." She spoke directly to Bryan, in a barely audible voice. "Anyway, Bryan, you're not the only one in here who has tried that stuff." She made the motion of running a knife across her arm. The effort of speaking seemed to drain her tiny body.

"Thanks, Sara, but, I could give a . . . well, anyway, thanks." Bryan addressed Sara, not taking his eyes off Dylan. "And I'm Bryan. And I've seen most of you around, obviously."

They went around the circle like that. Everyone said their name and some said more. There were only nine people in the group, ten if you counted Dr. Spahic, which Bryan did automatically.

He still needed the numbers to work. But now he only thought about even and odd in stressful situations—not like before, when they had been all that mattered.

Some of the kids appeared to know each other well. Some were loners. It reminded Bryan of high school. All the players were represented—the geeks, the cool kids, and the jocks—as usual, he didn't fit in anywhere.

Dr. Spahic didn't exactly lead the group, rather she ensured they stayed focused and in control. "I'm simply the mediator," she explained for Bryan's benefit. "We don't have many rules, but the ones we do have, we've all agreed to. But——" she raised her eyebrows at Dylan, "every so often, some people in the group tend to suffer a memory lapse."

'Simply mediating' meant shutting down Dylan about every three seconds, so that other people had a chance to say something. Only one person paid real attention to Dylan. A freckled red-haired girl who bit her fingernails nonstop, she hung on his every word, laughed at his attempts at humour and sneered on command. She had little to say for herself and seemed content to walk in Dylan's shadow. Bryan had seen the type before. He felt both contempt and sympathy for her. Every bully has a loyal dog, sort of like his mom acted around his dad. Not like Jessie. She had a mind of her own. She'd never minced words or held back her opinion with him.

"Does anyone have anything they'd like to say this morning? Who'd like to start?"

"I'd like to say that this is stupid and nothing ever comes of these sessions."

"You don't have to be here if you don't want to be here, Dylan."

He shrugged, "There's nothing else to do."

"You always say that and you are always here," pointed out Sara. "Why do you show up if you hate it so much?" In spite of her size, she challenged Dylan, and Bryan admired her courage.

"Maybe I'm an idiot."

"Maybe you are," she replied. "I can't think of any other explanation."

Bryan liked her even more. He couldn't help but laugh. "I second that."

"Okay, let's move on," Dr. Spahic demanded, as Dylan half rose from his seat. "You know the rules."

"We need a place where we can smoke," said another boy whose name Bryan had already forgotten.

"We've talked about this before, Clay. It's just not going to happen. For one thing, this is a hospital and for another you are too young, by law, to smoke."

"That's bullshit." Clay crossed his arms and kicked the leg of his chair. "My parents don't care if I smoke. They buy cigarettes for me when I tell them to."

"Perhaps. But that's the way it is. Rules aren't always made to keep people happy. Sometimes they are made to keep people safe."

"C-c-certain people h-h-hog the TV." A doughy-faced, overweight boy spoke softly, with a stutter, his eyes focused on the ground. Bryan strained to hear him. The boy, clearly terrified, refused to meet anybody's eyes. "I . . . I d-d-don't see w-why w-w-w-we can't have T-T-TVs in our own rooms."

"Does anyone else feel the same way that Joseph does?"

"I have no idea how he feels, because I didn't hear a word he said," Bryan said.

"S-s-sorry," Joseph stuttered to the room in general.

Dylan snickered. "I heard him and I don't think we need TVs in our rooms. I kind of like how things work in the common area."

He glared at Joseph. "You got a problem, Fat Boy?" He slammed his fist into the palm of his hand. "You want to talk about it later?"

"One more of those and you're out," said Dr. Spahic.

Sara spoke up. "How many people wish Dylan would leave?"

Everyone except Dr. Spahic, the red-haired girl and Bryan raised their hands. Bryan remained indifferent. One thing he knew for sure: sometimes it's better to let the drama play out without being a part of it.

"Don't worry." Dylan stood up. "I'm outta here," he snarled. He swaggered out of the room. The meek, red-haired girl scuttled after him.

"Later," someone muttered.

"I think Dylan felt uncomfortable enough that he did the right thing and left," Dr. Spahic offered. "By sticking together you were able to accomplish something important. Good job. Perhaps he'll think more about his behaviour the next time he's in the group."

As the session wore on, Bryan, in spite of efforts to remain indifferent to the discussions going on around him, found himself unwittingly drawn into the discussions between Dr. Spahic and the other 'patients.' Against his will, he began to feel more comfortable. He'd been wrong when he'd put all the kids in one category—the crazy category—and he'd been wrong again when he'd figured they'd all be boring. They weren't, and some of the things they shared about how they felt struck close to home. Although he remained silent, he felt a certain reassurance in the discovery that he wasn't the only person in the world who felt like an aberration. As the hour drew to a close, Dr. Spahic steered the conversation toward communication and they finished off the session by talking a little bit about group dynamics. "Great work," Dr. Spahic told them all. "Any questions, comments or queries can be e-mailed directly to me if they can't wait until the next time we meet."

As everyone dispersed, Bryan sensed that Sara wanted to talk to him, but he hung back until she had left. He did want to get to know her better, but he didn't feel quite ready to make a friend, not just yet.

That night he called his mother. When she answered the phone, he hung up. All of the things he'd wanted to say jammed in his throat. Still, it felt good to hear her voice.

"It's a beginning," Dr. Spahic said to him the next day when he told her what he had done. "Don't push yourself, you've already come a long way. How's the journaling coming along?"

"Okay."

"How do you feel about it?"

"Why do you always use the word 'feel'? I like the writing. I like having my guitar, but don't you get it yet? I don't feel—not since Michelle." He reached into his pocket and pulled out a piece of paper. "I like this band. I like how they put things. They get it. This is pretty much where I'm at. I can't do this today," he pleaded. "I'm sorry."

After he had left her office, Dr. Spahic unfolded the crumpled paper and read what Bryan had handed her. She stared at the lyrics for a long time before placing them in Bryan's growing file. Then she picked up the phone and dialed his home number. When Bryan's mother answered, Dr. Spahic spoke with more confidence than she felt. "Mrs. Bianchi, I know this will be hard for you, but I need you to tell me everything you can about the night your daughter died."

They spoke for nearly an hour. After the conversation, Dr. Spahic took a closer look at the lyrics that meant so much to Bryan. *Finally*, she thought, *I'm beginning to get somewhere.*

> *I'm pretty far gone but I'm still here*
> *Can nobody help me to disappear?*

Twenty-four

Bryan sat in the uncomfortable vinyl chair at his favourite place—in front of the windows overlooking the grounds. Everywhere he saw renewal—in the gardens filled with brightly coloured flowers, in the leafy green trees that formed a canopy over the walkways and in the cloudless blue sky. A groundskeeper pushed a mower up and down the long expanse of lawn, forming a perfect linear pattern in the grass. Bryan's eyes followed the groundskeeper's movements, but his thoughts were in the past. Every so often he tapped out sentences and sometimes paragraphs on his laptop. The summer sun streamed through the windowpanes and warmed his body. He was vaguely aware of the early morning hospital sounds, but nothing distracted him from his writing. He felt safe, safe enough, at least, to write freely. Yesterday, Dr. Spahic had encouraged him to really focus on the words he put down on the page. "When you're ready, I'd like you to share parts of your daily journal with me." She'd suggested this before, but only recently had he thought that at last he might be ready to do so.

At the last session he'd told her why he'd been deleting most of what he wrote: "I'm afraid of what I'm writing—of what I might find out."

"Don't worry," she said. "I promise. Once you discover what it is that has you so frightened, once you really focus on what it is that scares you, you will discover how to overcome it."

"What do you mean by 'really focus'?"

"Continue to free-write—to put down anything that comes to mind; but if you write something that makes you uncomfortable, explore it. It's like music. You pick up your guitar and play a few notes and if you like them, you fool around with the sound and, *voilà*—a new song."

"*Voilà*!" he laughed. "I wish it were that easy."

"Well, you know what I mean. Sure, it takes a bit of work . . ."

"If I try to do this, can I get out of this place?"

"It'll probably get you out a lot sooner," she replied. She spoke in a serious tone, a tone that gave Bryan hope. Dr. Spahic never said anything that she didn't mean. "But, before you leave, you'll have to be able to face the people who care about you. Your mom's just waiting for the okay from me, and Jessie has asked if she can visit."

"Jessie? Are you sure?" He felt himself colour. He began to pick at an invisible loose thread in his jeans. "Jessie?"

"Yes, Jessie. Would you like to see her?"

"I'm so not ready for that. I mean, I broke up with her. She hates me. You wouldn't believe what a jerk I've been to her."

"I anticipated your answer, and I told her I didn't think you'd agree." She paused to let her words sink in. "So she dropped this off for you." She held out a plain white envelope addressed to him. "You can read it now or after our session. Your choice."

He took the envelope in trembling hands. "I'd rather open it when I'm alone," he breathed.

When Bryan returned to his room, he shut the door, tore open the letter and began to read:

Dear Bryan,

First of all, I don't play guitar. I never wanted your guitar, and I'm thankful every day that it remains yours and not mine. ☺ Your mom told me you can't get e-mail in the hospital, so I've dropped off this note to your doctor—who seems like a pretty okay lady.

I think I know, maybe more than anyone, how awful the past two years have been for you. I want you to know, I miss our friendship—a lot. I realize we are broken up, but does that mean we can never speak to each other again? Please agree to see me, and please get well quickly.

Your good friend,
Jessie

He read and reread her short note over and over again, until he'd memorized it. Then he folded it carefully and placed it in his bedside-table drawer. Why didn't she hate him? None of it made any sense, but he knew that he felt better than he had in a long time. Dr. Spahic had told him he could get out earlier if he started writing things down and sharing them with her. Without hesitation, he grabbed his laptop, and began to type:

All in all, Michelle's funeral was pretty good. I recognized every-one, all the aunts and uncles, and the cousins I never see except at disasters and celebrations. The neighbours were there as well. Dad's colleagues from the university, some of his grad students, Mom's friends from work, Michelle's friends from school, my friends, and Jessie and her family, of course.

Jessie, the only one who knows the entire truth.

I've been to a couple of funerals; Grandma Nelson and my Grandpa Bianchi on Dad's side. None of my grandparents are alive. More disappeared people. Poor Michelle. I hope she meets some more exciting souls, wherever she is.

Anyway, I thought those funerals were kind of boring . . . but at least at my grandfather's funeral Michelle and I got into the liquor and nobody noticed, even though we got really pissed. I threw up in the back garden, behind the cedar tree. Michelle stood a few feet away, on guard, splitting a gut. "You need to learn to hold your booze, Bry."

She always called me Bry, or Little Bro, or Dumb Ass—but always in fun, if you know what I mean. Most of the time, I didn't care. I knew she didn't mean anything by it.

I guess, looking back, that funeral was pretty fun. I wasn't that attached to my grandfather. He reminded me of my father, only meaner, shorter and thinner-lipped. Michelle made a toast to Grandfather, while she smoked the cigarette I'd stolen from Uncle Luke's pack. "Good riddance, you old bugger," I think is what she said. Good thing nobody heard us. Mom would have killed us if she heard us talking like that.

"I don't know why everyone's crying," Michelle said. "Don't you think that people that old must want to die?"

I'd never actually thought about it before. "How old was he?"

"I don't know. I bet he was seventy. Who cares? Old is old. Thirty is old. Shit, seventeen feels old most of the time. I don't want to live past twenty. God, what I am I supposed to do, get married, have a bunch of kids and work my ass off? Nope, twenty is a good age to die."

I didn't really like it when Michelle talked like that. I guess deep down I knew she meant it.

I thought about that a lot—the age thing. Do people actually get so old that they want to die? Of course that was before I saw any appeal in kickin' it.

Now I get it.

I never cried at my grandparents' funerals. I didn't cry at Michelle's. Weird, huh? I mean you'd think a normal person would cry if their sister died, but I didn't. It wasn't that I was being brave or anything. I just didn't feel like crying. It felt surreal, like I was watching a movie and in it at the same time.

Come to think of it, Mom didn't cry either. She'd taken a lot of drugs so she could keep calm and make sure all the guests were

comfortable. Dad said, "I don't want a scene. This is bad enough
without hysterics."

Dad's too practical. Mom isn't. Those two are so different. I wonder what they saw in each other in the first place.

I guess I'm more like Mom. Once I heard Dad yell, "Sometimes
I wonder if he is my son!" I know he was accusing her of messing
around with some other guy, but I can't see her ever doing something like that. I guess he just couldn't face knowing that I'm his
flesh and blood. I don't blame him, not all the time anyway.

I had bruises all over me at Michelle's funeral. Bruises from the
accident. I hadn't been out of the hospital for long, so I got a lot
of sympathy, even though I'm guessing everyone thought I'd got
what I deserved. Who am I to tell them the truth? Let Michelle
rest in peace with her reputation intact. That's the least I can do
for her, as a brother. While everyone was downstairs crying and
stuff, I took Michelle's guitar from the living room and put it on
its stand in her room. It hasn't moved to this day. It's better that
way. That guitar is a world of trouble.

She would have been pissed off if she'd heard the music they'd
chosen for the service. I bet she'd never even heard most of the
songs—well, except for "I Did It My Way," which, as Michelle
said, "totally lacks imagination. At my funeral," she'd mused,
almost as an afterthought, but I wonder about that now, "I want

them to play songs like 'Highway to Hell' or 'Wish You Were Here.' " Funny at the time, or had she been giving me a hint? I'd forgotten all about that conversation . . .

For a while I had to stand in the receiving line, sandwiched between Mom and Dad. All those stupid comments from all those well-meaning people:

> She was a fine young woman . . .
> We'll all miss her . . .
> Our thoughts are with you . . .
> Time will heal all . . .
> God works in mysterious ways . . .
> Thank goodness you still have one child left . . .

That last one was a real joke, but you wouldn't believe how many times I heard it. Usually the idiot talking would turn to me and lay a gentle hand on my shoulder. Eventually, I told them I was too sore to stand there with broken ribs, and I left.

At the time, it kind of worried me that I wasn't crying or feeling much at all. Come to think of it, that was the first time I ever burned myself. I didn't feel that either.

The funeral was the last fun day we had together as a family. By 'fun' I mean there were guests and music and lots of food. Since then, we haven't had too many people over. I think they drop by to be nice, but it's obvious they figure out pretty quickly that none of us are in the mood for visitors.

It would have been a perfect party—if Michelle had been there.

Twenty-five

I saw Mom today. Dr. Spahic told me that she has been to the hospital a lot and that she's in counseling! I agreed to see her because I want out of here, and I don't think they'll ever let me go if I can't at least talk to my own mother.

Plus, I kind of wanted to see her.

Sara got out. I knew she was the most normal of us all. It turns out she is anorexic—but anyone could have guessed that. She had to put on a certain amount of weight, and keep it on, to get out of here. I hope she makes it. Since I made a point of not getting to know her, I'm okay about her leaving. Just proves my point: don't get attached to people, and they can't hurt you.

I didn't ask Mom about Dad, and she didn't bring him up, but Dr. Spahic did. Trust her to always leap into the shit pile.

Anyway, that's how I found out that Dad has gone away to Asia on a sabbatical. And all this time, I thought he didn't care about me—heh-heh. At first I thought, It's funny that Mom didn't go with him, but then the light bulb went on, and I thought, They don't like each other. I bet this is the beginning of the end for them. Worse yet, I didn't care. In fact, I had the opposite feeling. I hoped the old bastard was gone for good. Even though Mom would never say it, I'm pretty sure she felt the same way. It's all speculation. I'll find out for sure when I get out.

Anyway, Mom looked better. Less pallid . . . She said we had a lot to talk about, but it could wait until I set the whole thing in motion. Little does she know just how much we have to talk about. I guess one day I'll tell her the truth about Michelle, but not now. I'm still not sure exactly what the truth is.

✕

I got kicked out of group therapy. I punched Dylan, but he deserved it. Asshole. Group therapy—what a waste of time. I'm not allowed back until I apologize, so I guess I won't be going back there in this lifetime. Dr. Spahic really called it wrong on this one. Why would or should I apologize to a bully?

People suck.

Most of them, anyway.

Apparently, there was some problem with the anti-depressant I was taking when I tried to off myself. Dr. Spahic told me all about it. Now, the government has recommended that no one under eighteen should be taking Zeldox—it might make them prone to killing themselves.

lol

The new drug I'm on seems better, but they have to keep me here until they are sure it doesn't have any side effects—like suicide. I don't even know what it is they're giving me, but I can't sleep at night, I'm itchy all the time and my mouth feels like a desert. But, for a while, it didn't bother me at all.

Sweet. I don't even know how long I've been in this place. A month? Two months? More? Less? The trees are heavy and green, as Michelle would have said. I'm ready to go home.

It's my birthday today. We had cake in the common room. There was no hidden file inside the cake to saw my way out of here—so I'm still here . . .

Everyone sang Happy Birthday.

Is this supposed to make me feel good?

✕

I forgot to mention that Jessie gave Mom a birthday card to give to me. She made it herself. She has always been pretty artistic. She never gives up on me. Sometimes I like her for this and at other times I hate her.

✕

I remember parts of that night—the night that Michelle bit it. I remember the sweet smell of gasoline. I used to like that smell. I remember the blood creeping over the surface of the road toward me; a growing pool of red on black. I remember the rain bouncing off my face as I lay there waiting for someone to do something. There are more memories locked away in the recesses of my mind. They are resurfacing every day or in my dreams at night.

Dr. Spahic says I'm the only one who holds the key to them. I told Dr. Spahic what I remembered so far and she seemed pleased. I don't have to look at Michelle's picture so often now. I keep the photo in the drawer beside my bed, and I look at it when I can't remember her face, or when I can only picture her in pieces on the road. She looked like a broken doll.

After several disappointments, the new meds are working. Dr. Spahic is starting to talk about me being on the outside. Funny isn't it? I've got nothing to look forward to, but I can't wait to get out of here.

I'm free! For whatever reason, I got my walking papers today. I never want to go back to that place again. Mom picked me up before lunch, and now I'm back home in my bedroom. I had to sign a contract to get out. "Just in case," said Dr. Spahic. "If you ever feel like you are backsliding, read it. I trust you to keep your word."

Weird. Not many people trust me. Jessie did once. Michelle did, too, I guess.

Anyway, I signed my name and promised: no cutting, no drinking and no drugs. I promised to continue to keep my appointments with Dr. Spahic once a week. I'm allowed to finish off grade twelve by correspondence. I promised to keep on writing. Not that I could quit if I wanted to.

I'm addicted to my own words.

✕

Dad is not coming home, not for a while at least. He's going to fin-ish off his sabbatical in Asia. Mom is much happier. She doesn't miss him at all. She hasn't said so, but I can tell.

I don't miss him either.

You would think that with only two of us in the house, we would be lonely, but things are going pretty well. I'm not complaining. I showed Mom the scars all over my body, and she bit her lower lip and did her best not to cry. I told her it didn't matter to me if she leaked a few tears, and that made her laugh. We hugged and it felt natural.

Michelle was right about Mom. She doesn't understand, not really, but she is trying. I almost told her about Michelle, but I stopped myself in time. I'm not sure if it's Mom who can't face the truth or me?

I'm not bored like I thought I would be. I do my schoolwork, play guitar, listen to music, and actually hang a bit with Mom. She's learning not to hover. I'm learning not to mind.

It's working okay.

Twenty-six

Dr. Spahic told him straight up: "You're going to have good days and you are going to have bad days." So far Bryan had been cruising somewhere between the two extremes. She advised him to prepare himself for the lows, to build up some defenses. And he thought he had.

Wrong.

Wrong.

Wrong.

The sucker punch came just when everything seemed to be going reasonably well. Bryan and his mom had settled into a comfortable, quiet routine and although Bryan wasn't exactly happy, he wasn't miserable either.

It happened at the grocery store about a month after he returned home. He never saw it coming. He was standing in front of the bread trying to figure out which brand he should buy. What did they eat at home? He looked at the list his mother had given him. It just said 'whole wheat bread,' but there must have been thirty different brand names, and none of them looked the same, and none of them looked familiar. He picked up one and dropped it into the half-full shopping cart.

Then he heard her laughing.

He froze. Would know that sound anywhere . . .

He pulled his hoodie down over his forehead and looked around hopelessly. Nowhere to hide. He prepared to bolt. *The coward's way out.* Too late. She had spotted him. *This is what they mean by looking like a deer caught in headlights*, he thought, feeling as his heart might burst out of his chest.

Jessie moved into his line of vision and planted herself firmly in front of him. "Hi, Bryan."

"Hi, Jess," his voice cracked. *God, I sound pathetic*. He tried again, "Hi, Jess!" Now he sounded like he was yelling at her. He shoved his sticky, wet hands into his pockets and tried to breathe normally. If there were a God, a hole would open in the floor and swallow him up.

No choice, so he did the only thing he could. He turned to her, his emotions all over the map, his eyes downcast. Happy to see her, scared to see her, wishing he could speak, wishing he could disappear.

"It's good to see you," she said, rescuing him. She sounded genuine. "I mean, I heard you got out, and I've been waiting for you to call me. It really is great to see you. You look excellent."

"Good to see you, too." He heard the hesitation his voice and hoped that she didn't.

"You don't sound very convincing," she giggled. "You never were a very good bullshitter, Bryan."

"I guess I'm not that used to chitchat anymore."

She rolled her green eyes and planted a friendly punch on his shoulder, laughing. "Yeah, like you ever had that skill!"

He started laughing, too. "I know. I know . . . I guess I sort of owe you an apology—you know—for everything."

"I guess you do," she joked. "Anyway, I'm gonna go and let you keep shopping . . ." She seemed suddenly uncomfortable, more nervous than he was.

He didn't want her to leave. "Maybe we could go for a coffee? I'm almost finished," he lied.

Her eyes darted back and forth. "I'd like to. Really I would, but . . . well, I can't right now . . ." She began to back away, and she was almost at the end of the aisle when a tall guy appeared behind her.

"You disappeared," he said to her. "We gotta get going, or we'll miss our ride." He strode to her side.

"Yeah. Sorry, I ran into an old friend." She gestured toward Bryan. "This is Brad," she mumbled. "Brad, this is Bryan."

So, she wasn't alone. *Brad could be a cousin, or a friend. Don't jump to conclusions. Just because she is with a guy doesn't mean she is* with *him. Just because he is standing two centimetres away from her doesn't mean a thing.*

Nobody knows you and nobody wants to.

Shut up, voice. He stopped himself from covering his ears. *Nobody knows you and nobody wants to.* They'd got that line right. He should get the lyric tattooed on his arm.

"Hey." Brad nodded and hooked his left arm proprietarily around

Jessie's waist. Jessie squirmed, but that only served to make everything worse.

Spiralling down. Bryan tried to appear cool, unaffected, and nonchalant, as if he didn't feel like someone had taken a knife and stuck it in his gut, as if she hadn't reached into his chest and ripped his heart out with her bare hands. Brad put out his hand to shake with Bryan. It killed him, but he stuck out his hand to meet Brad's. "Nice to meet you."

Liar, liar, liar.

They stood there, and no one said a word, for what felt like forever. Finally Jessie spoke up. "So, anyway. Um, we should get together. You know, catch up . . ."

"Yeah, well I've been busy. It looks like you have been, too." He knew he wasn't being fair. He sounded so hostile, so hurt, so fucking wounded. He clenched his fists by his side. He didn't have any claim on her. What had he expected? That she would wait around forever for a loser?

The guy, whatever the fuck his name was, didn't say a word. He stood there smirking, and why not? He had Jessie.

She shuffled from foot to foot, and her dark hair swung over her eyes. Finally she broke the heavy silence that lay between them.

"I guess I'll see you around," she said. "Or not."

Stop standing there in front of them like an idiot. Say something, anything. Bryan cleared his throat. He sniffled. His lips raised in the imitation of a smile that made it impossible to cross the distance between them. "I'm picking up some groceries."

Stupid, stupid, stupid.

"Us, too," Jessie replied.

The asshole cleared his throat, and smiled. "Well . . . we're in a *grocery store*," he said and squeezed Jessie. "Well, I guess that pretty much covers everything. Come on, babe, let's go."

For the first time since he'd punched out Dylan, Bryan wanted to kill someone more than he wanted to kill himself. *Don't go,* he longed to tell her. Instead, he said, "Later," but his feet were rooted to the floor.

"Bye, Bryan." Jessie touched his arm gently. "Say hi to your mom."

"Okay," he answered. "I'll do that."

"Good. See you around . . . I'm glad you're back."

Had he heard regret or relief in her voice? Was she really glad he was back? He watched her walk away on the arm of her idiot boyfriend. His eyes followed her until the two of them had disappeared down another aisle. For a long time he stood staring at the shelves of bread, then he left the cart in the aisle and walked out of the store empty-handed. He walked the streets aimlessly until his feet led him home.

His mom stood on the front porch, wringing her hands. "What's happened, Bryan? I've been worried sick . . . Come inside and we'll have a cup of tea."

"What happened?" she repeated once they were in the kitchen.

"Nothing. Nothing happened, Mom. Oh, except I forgot the groceries."

"That's okay, honey."

"I got confused about the bread."

She looked at him, her eyes fearful. "Is it only about bread?"

He hated himself for upsetting her. He hated the bad in him. The part that wouldn't allow him to apologize. The part that kept screwing up.

Tell her you are sorry.
But I'm not.
I'm not anything.

Tell her the truth.
But I can't.
I don't know what is truth and what is imagined.

Then make something up.
Why do you have to drag everyone down with you?
Easy. I've been inventing my feelings for as long as I've lived.

"I'm not feeling so great, that's all, Mom. It's nothing to worry about. I think I'm just gonna go to bed."

"It's barely eight o'clock." The kettle whistled. "At least have a cup of tea or a snack?"

"Mom. All I want to do is to sleep. Nothing else."

"You'll tell me, won't you? I mean if . . ."

He saved her from finishing the sentence. "I'll tell you, Mom."

Would I?

In the bathroom, he found the razor exactly where he had left it so many months ago. He held it in his hand for a long time. Old friend. Painkiller. He pressed it into the flesh on his forearms, and ran it over the scar tissue on his stomach. He touched it to his calves and held it to his throat, but he didn't cut, didn't even break skin. *I don't need you, old friend.* He replaced the razor in the bathroom cupboard, closed the door and left the room.

He didn't want go back there, not even over Jessie, but he didn't want to be here either.

He didn't want to be.

At least he had music. He picked up his guitar and began to play. He played until his fingers ached. He sang his best Nomeansno tune, and the whole time he thought about Jessie and her asshole boyfriend.

> *What I want most in the whole wide world*
> *is a girl just a girl one who will keep me*
> *from losing my mind*

Was it too much to ask?

Twenty-seven

Where, Bryan considered, is the magic spot where most people seemed to negotiate their daily lives? For months now, Dr. Spahic had been trying to help him find that place. Sometimes he got it, but most of the time it eluded him.

"You have to be very courageous to live a full life," she'd said at one point, and those words had stuck with him. Maybe being courageous had something to do with honesty. For sure, it had a lot to do with trust. He wanted a full life and he knew he had to start somewhere.

So, three days after his encounter with Jessie in the grocery store, he e-mailed her.

To: Jess@onet.ca
Subject: R U still talking to me?

Jess,

I'll bet you're surprised to hear from me after the other day in the store. Not as surprised as me. You were right, I'm doing better, but I've got a ways to go. I know what you want me to do, and I will, when I'm ready. I guess what I'm saying is that I could use a little help.

I could use a friend.

Never thought I'd hear myself say those words.

It's too bad about the boyfriend, but I hope you are happy. (I guess.)

BTW I'm not cutting anymore.
Bryan

After rereading the e-mail a thousand times, he pushed SEND. It turned out to be one of the most difficult things he had done in a long, long time. He didn't know if she'd reply, but if she didn't, he'd taken the risk, and that alone filled him with pride. An hour later, he checked his inbox and, to his astonishment, she'd responded.

To: Bryan_Bianchi@onet.ca
Subject: re: R U still talking to me?

Bryan,

OMG, it's great to hear from you at last. I'd sort of given up on us, but I still think about you all the time.

I don't know what happened, how we grew so far apart, but of course I am here for you. It's not going to be easy, what you have to do, but I will stand by you. On your time . . .

The cutting sucked.

My boyfriend is a good guy, but kind of boring.

Call me,
Jessie

PS. I didn't want your guitar that badly.

Bryan thought, *She hasn't totally dumped me. Is this what hope feels like?*

That afternoon, he stood at the top of the stairs and listened to laughter, the newest sound in their house. Downstairs, Stella and Mom were talking nonstop. He couldn't hear their exact words, only the obvious pleasure in their voices. He worried about what would happen between them when his father returned home.

Would everything go back to how it had been?

He talked to Dr. Spahic about it the next time he saw her. He'd gone back to meeting her in her house once he'd left the hospital. He liked being in her comfortable, messy office—in the midst of her organized chaos; entertained by the antics of the cats he'd come to love.

Once he'd settled into his favourite chair, he began. "I have these daydreams. They're a little warped."

"That's why they are called daydreams," she replied. "If you act on them, without thinking them through, then it becomes warped. Until then, it's harmless. In fact it is quite healthy. Want to tell me about them? Look at that! I think Kody missed you! Give her a little push, if she's distracting you."

"She's okay. Anyway, sometimes, when things are going really well at home, you know, when Mom is happy and stuff, I think about how great it would be if something happened to Dad."

"What kind of something?"

"You know. The fatal kind of something. Heart attack, train crash, wrong-place-at-wrong-time type scenario. He could choke on a chicken bone, or pick up some tropical disease, or get hit by a runaway bus, or some Darwin-award type death, you know, like that guy who Krazy-Glued himself to a rhinoceros's butt and suffocated on its shit."

A ghost of a smile played on Dr. Spahic's lips. "I haven't heard that one, but go on."

"I imagine Mom and me getting the phone call, or whatever. You know, a cop comes to the door and tells us that Dad has become one of the disappeared people. We cry and pretend to be really traumatized, and Stella hugs us, and then we carry on, and everything is good."

"Uh-huh?"

"You know, there is a funeral and we are sort of sad, but not really. Oh, and I pick the music."

She raised her eyebrows, clearly puzzled, but let it go. "So things are different, better at your house now that your dad is gone?"

"The tension is gone. Mom has a friend and actually, she's our housekeeper. Stella . . . she used to be my . . . our nanny. Mom laughs and talks with Stella, like they used to when we . . . when I . . . when we were kids. I don't obsess on even and odd numbers hardly at all. Mom goes into Michelle's room less. She's even given away some of her clothes to Stella's daughter, and she's donated a few things to the Salvation Army." Bryan hesitated. "She doesn't blame me for what happened to Michelle. She doesn't drink much either."

"Let's get back to the whole fault issue. I want you to think about other ways you can deal with your feelings about your dad besides killing him off."

"There are no other ways." He half-laughed. "It's either kill him off or cut him out." Unexpected tears forced him to bury his head in his hands and close his eyes. Kody rubbed herself against his leg, and he let the tears flow. Dr. Spahic sat quietly and when he had cried himself out, she handed him a tissue.

"Show me your scars." Dr. Spahic spoke firmly, catching Bryan off guard.

He blew his nose and frowned at her. "I'm not a freak, you know. Besides, you examined me—in the hospital the night I was admitted. You've seen them. Why pretend you haven't?"

"I want you to be a part of this. It's important that you show me. When I examined you, you were unconscious."

Bryan stood up and pulled up his shirt to expose his stomach. He'd never voluntarily exposed his cut-up body to anyone. He watched Dr. Spahic like a hawk, wanting to gauge her reaction. He rolled up his sleeves and shoved his arms at her. "Are you happy now? That's the only way I know how to deal with anything. Is that what you wanted to hear? Did you want me to admit it?"

Dr. Spahic didn't flinch, and her eyes never wavered in disgust. Nor did her face register the expected shock or the repulsion. He saw empathy, not pity, in her wise expression and knowing eyes. His guard dropped—plummeted to the ground—and he dropped his arms to his side and started to sob, more like a three-year-old kid than a teenager. She proffered the box of tissues, once again, and when he'd composed himself, she continued as if nothing had happened. "What did you feel before you hurt yourself?"

"I don't remember. Nothing, I guess. I felt nothing."

"Look at these pictures." She held up a sheet of different smilies. Their expressions ranged from euphoric to devastated. "I understand that you felt nothing, but if you had to pick one emotion, what would it be? Just point to one."

Bryan wiped his nose with the sleeve of his shirt and studied the diagrams. Some he didn't recognize. *Do people really feel all those things?* "That one." He pointed to an image whose mouth twisted downward and whose eyes flashed.

"Do you know what that is?" Dr. Spahic encouraged.

"Maybe. I guess anger."

"That's correct. That is the face of rage. Do you think that is perhaps how you felt before you cut yourself?"

"Something like that."

"Now I want you to think about this carefully. What did you feel after you cut yourself?"

"I don't have to think about that. I felt as if I existed; I felt human."

"Can you think of any other way of responding to rage, other than hurting yourself?"

"Hurting someone else." *Now she'll see what kind of a person I am.*

"Anything else?"

"Getting high. Getting drunk. Breaking something. I guess it's pretty obvious, I don't cope."

"Okay. That's good. You're thinking. We'll leave it at that for now. We've got a little time left, and I'd like to touch on the subject of your sister's death, her accident."

Bryan nodded. He'd seen this coming for a long time.

"You claim it was your fault. Why do you think you are to blame?"

"Everyone thinks so. I mean, she was picking me up the night she died. She didn't want to. She wanted to be at home, but they said I couldn't go out if she didn't. And I begged her to. I made her go out."

"So that makes it your fault?" Dr. Spahic leaned forward. "That doesn't really make sense to me," she said. "Can you explain further, so that I can understand?"

"They all thought Michelle was perfect. She wasn't, you know."

"Nobody is, Bryan. People make their own choices. What choice did your sister make that night?"

Did she know? Sometimes Bryan thought that she did. Other times he believed she was fishing; that she'd dropped her hook deep into his subconscious.

"Has anyone ever asked you to keep a secret?" he asked.
"Sure, lots of times. Part of my job is keeping secrets."

"Do you ever betray them?" Bryan asked quietly.

" 'Betray' is an interesting choice of words. Usually, if I think it is important enough that they reveal their secret, I help them come to that conclusion, so that they can reveal it themselves."

"What if you couldn't ask them?"

"Then I guess I would have to trust my own judgment." Dr. Spahic sounded confident, strong.

"I guess that's the difference between me and you. I don't trust anything about myself, or anyone else, come to think of it."

"I thought you trusted your friend Jessie?"

Bryan pictured her standing arm in arm with her boyfriend. "I used to," he said, "and I want to again. We're talking—on e-mail."

"Okay. That's good. That's really good." In the few minutes they had left, Dr. Spahic steered the conversation back to his daydreams about his father. "Bryan, I'd like you to consider asking your mom how she feels about your dad returning home."

I don't have to respond. I just have to listen and think about it later.

"I'd also like you to try to write down in your journal some of the ways you might cope when someone or something makes you angry."

Silence.

She leaned back in her chair and picked some of the cat hair off the armrest, waiting for a reply.

I can wait you out.

After what seemed like forever, Bryan gave in. *Doesn't she have other crazies to see? Does she plan to just sit here all day waiting on me? What does she expect from me?* "You might be content to sit here all day, but I've got stuff to do," he said.

"You're free to leave any time you want. I know how difficult it is for you to verbalize how you feel. You've been amazing today."

"About what you asked me do, I'll think about it, but I'm not making any guarantees."

Twenty-eight

"Mom!" Bryan called softly into the darkness, but instinct told him the house lay empty. "Mom?" He raised his voice. "Are you home?" The luminescent face of his watch read 8:30 p.m. She should be home.

He stood in the kitchen unused to being alone and not liking it. The dim light from the streetlamp outside the window cast a pale glow across the room. The things that were so familiar in the daytime were suddenly alien, leaving Bryan feeling helpless and inexplicably nervous. He'd come to depend on his mother since coming home from the hospital, and they had an unspoken agreement that she wouldn't leave him alone. They'd never discussed it—they both knew how difficult it was for Bryan to admit his fear of being at home alone.

He looked around the kitchen, chiding himself for his insecurity,

but it did no good. The shadows from the stove and fridge mor-
phed into otherworldly beings—ominous, threatening. *I'm
behaving like I'm five years old.*

*Sound memory, unwelcome: He doesn't need a nightlight. You're
turning him into a sissy.*

"Mom!" he called again, adding a little more volume.

He thought he'd expunged the old, familiar demon, but no. It
had just been dormant in the pit of his stomach for all this time.
He braced himself mentally, knowing it had already begun to
stir. Soon it would worm its way through his body, increasing his
heart rate and cutting off his airway. He recognized the increasing panic. *What had Dr. Spahic said? Think. We talked about
coping. Stop and breathe. Count slowly backward from ten to one.
Do it again if you have to. Try to stay focused in the present.*

*Mom must be somewhere. Just because she is not here does not
mean she has disappeared. It just means she is late getting home.*
"Mom?"

Bryan knew that if he didn't move, he wouldn't be able to keep
the demon at bay. It took a huge amount of effort to come un-
glued from the floor. He walked over to the drawer where they
kept the butcher knife. *To protect myself,* he lied. He opened the
unyielding drawer slowly.

Maybe she has left this place?
Maybe she has left me?
Who could blame her?

The blade's edge flashed at him in the muted light. Bryan reached for it. *Old friend.* It lay nestled on its side—cold comfort. He reached in and stroked the steel softly. All he had to do to feel safer was to take it from its place in the drawer and hold it against his skin. No! *What else can you do when you are afraid or angry?* he heard Dr. Spahic's voice asking. *Recognize what you are feeling. Tell yourself what you are feeling.*

I'm afraid. I'm all alone. I hate the dark. Nobody loves me. I sure don't. Emotion: fear. I am afraid.

What else can you do?

Light. Sound.

He closed the drawer slowly and moved, zombie-like, to the light switch. He snapped it on and drew in a huge breath—relief. "Ten, nine, eight, seven..." The kitchen transformed from the hostile, eerie place it had been a second before to the room he had known all his life. "Six, five, four..." he continued for good measure. "Three, two, one." He opened the fridge, pulled out the carton of milk and began to drink, focusing on the sensation of the cold fluid sliding down his throat.

I can feel this.
I am here.
I don't have to cut.

The milk tasted good. In the silence, he congratulated himself. Then he heard something that caused him to freeze on the spot. Directly above his head, in Michelle's old room, he distinctly heard movement. For a moment he rejoiced: *Michelle is home!*

Impossible.

A ribbon of fear wrapped around his throat and began to tighten. He dropped the carton of milk, and it exploded at his feet. Bryan looked around him wildly. Time had not only stopped, it was sliding backwards. *Michelle is home!* His eyes darted nervously between the knife drawer and the puddle of milk. His feet might as well have been encased in concrete. From above him came the plaintive notes of one of Michelle's favourite songs—Metallica's cover of Led Zeppelin's "Stairway to Heaven." He shook his head, tried to expel the notes, but they leaked through the ceiling to the kitchen, to him. He wiped his sweaty palms against his jeans, couldn't move.

She's my sister. There is nothing to be afraid of. Dead people can't hurt me. It's not possible. He recoiled and bumped the counter, sending a mug crashing to the floor. And he choked back a terrified moan. Later, he had no memory of how he got to the stairs, but he approached them tentatively, leaving milky footprints in his wake. With each step the sounds amplified. He hesitated at the top, wanted to bolt, but he forced himself forward. *It's either this or the knife.*

He'd expected Michelle's door to be open, but it wasn't. He took a minute to find his courage, and then he reached out and gripped the glass doorknob. A bead of perspiration rolled down his face, and then another. He took a deep breath and turned the doorknob slowly, pushing the door open, Michelle's name on the tip of his tongue.

Mom!

Either she hadn't heard him enter the room, or she chose to ignore him. He stared at her back. She was sitting on the floor surrounded by piles of things that had belonged to Michelle. She hadn't seen him yet. He cleared his throat, "Mom, what's going on? What are you doing?" He didn't recognize his own voice—heard only fear.

She started at the sound of his voice, but didn't turn around.

If I could just see her face . . . . Is she okay? Has she lost it?

As if reading his mind, she spoke. "Don't worry. It's okay. I'm okay. I'm doing what should have been done a long time ago. I'm going through your sister's stuff. I'm listening to the music she loved." She shrugged. She didn't appear sad so much as somehow different.

"I don't understand it," she said. "I've tried, but I don't get it."

"Understand what, Mom?" Not taking his eyes off her for a second, Bryan ventured slowly into the bedroom and planted himself in front of her. "What, Mom?" he said in a gentle voice—the same gentle voice she'd used on him when he'd been so scared.

"Her music. But then I never bothered to listen, did I?" She continued speaking almost to herself; she didn't see Bryan, she saw a memory. "Your dad hated the music and I never had the chance to actually listen. He would be furious if he saw me now, sitting here amidst all Shell's stuff listening to this music. Headbanger music, he called it. He said it was noise. Meaningless noise. Imagine that."

"Yeah, that sounds like Dad."

Finally she turned to face him. "It does, doesn't it? People change over the years."

"Who changed, Mom? Michelle never changed," Bryan said. "She just sort of . . ."

"No, I mean your dad. He changed, you know, right after Michelle was born. I think the whole idea of a family scared him." She picked up one of Michelle's old T-shirts and ran her fingers over the logo on the front. "What does this mean— 'Nomeansno'? Was she having problems with a boy?"

Bryan smiled in spite of everything. "Not really, Mom. It's the name of a band. And I think it means, 'Listen to me the first time,' you know? I think it means the world isn't always such a great place, but sometimes it's all right. As far as I know, Michelle was pretty good with the guys."

"It's time for us to rid this house of all its ghosts," she said.

"Mom." Bryan squatted on the floor beside her. "Mom, I'll help you." He touched her shoulder. "You don't have to do this by yourself."

There were questions Bryan had to ask, things he needed to know. Now seemed like the right time to talk to her. "When is Dad coming home?"

"You have milk all over your shoes, and you're shaking."
"I'm okay, Mom."
"I suppose you're hungry."
"Sort of."
"We'll order something in."

"Great. Are you going to tell me about Dad?"

"Your dad hated to order in. Sounds crazy, doesn't it? It doesn't really matter what he thinks anymore." She sighed, but it wasn't a sigh of despair. "There are certain things a mother shouldn't have to say to her son and a son shouldn't have to listen to. That said, would it be terrible for you if he didn't return? You talked about honesty. It's your turn. Tell me the truth."

"Ah, truth. I'm not so good at that." He searched through Michelle's CDs until he found Nomeansno. "Listen to the lyrics." His hand still trembling, he ejected Metallica, inserted the new CD and pressed PLAY.

> *I've been lying to myself, lying to myself and it can't go on*
> *'Cause I'm lying in state, I've been lying in a state of grace*
> *I'm lying in state*
> *I'm lying to myself and can't go on*

She closed her eyes and listened. When the song was over, she reached out and took Bryan's hand. A tear rolled down her cheek. "Beneath all that noise, it actually says a lot. I'm sorry," she said. "I've really messed things up. I want to hear your truth."

"My truth . . . I hope he never comes back," said Bryan. "At least when Michelle was here, she protected me. That's why Dad liked Michelle better. She never showed her fear."

"I suppose, in a way, she did the job I should have done. She protected us both. Then she left. Sometimes I think Michelle chose to go."

Of course, this is the moment when I should tell her everything. I am a coward, though. I have lied for so long.

Mrs. Bianchi continued. "Dr. Spahic has been helping me to understand self-injury. One of the things she told me is that sometimes, if children are heavily criticized, if they feel helpless, they will hurt themselves. I knew what she meant . . . I should have protected you."

"Mom, I used to think that, but I don't want to blame you anymore. I guess you did the best you could. Mom, I'm not mad at you anymore. Now, about Dad? I need to know."

"I don't think your dad is coming back. I mean, to live here with us. It's been so hard." She turned to Bryan and smiled. "I'm sorry, honey. I wish I felt sad about it. Instead, I feel like I'm melting. It's as if I've been frozen for so long, and I'm finally fluid again. I want to go through Michelle's things. You must take what you want, I'll keep what I want, and the rest will go to someone who needs it."

"I don't think your dad is coming back." She could be talking about a teacher, or the guy who runs the corner store.

Bryan's eyes moved automatically to the guitar.

"Take it," said his mother. "She would want you to have it. Take the CDs as well. I know you bought a lot of them together. Take the vinyl, too. Who knows, maybe we can find an old turntable." Bryan hesitated.

"Now. Tonight," she said. "It's time—before I lose my courage."

Bryan watched as his mother took the soccer trophies down from the shelves one by one. She wrapped them in newspaper and placed them carefully in a box and wrote MICHELLE'S TROPHIES across the top. "I'll just put these in the attic," she said, "I'm not ready to let them go." But she wasn't talking to him anymore.

Next, she carefully took the posters down from the wall and rolled each one, securing them with elastic bands. Michelle had been big into skating, and a lot of the posters were signed by the top North American skaters. His mom looked each one over before packing it away in the cardboard box that she had lovingly marked, MICHELLE'S THINGS.

It occurred to Bryan that he'd never really seen his mother before. Not like this. He took Michelle's Rosa Hurricane and carried it to his own room. She smiled at him as he stepped over her. He took the vinyl collection and most of the CDs and then rejoined his mother. Together they went through Michelle's shirts. He chose the ones he liked and they made a separate pile for charity. "Is this too hard for you?" he asked his mother when they had sorted through all the clothes.

"I'm fine," she said to him. "I'm better than I've been in a long time. You don't have to worry about me anymore. I love you," she added. "And I'm sorry."

"I love you, too, Mom."

She blew him a kiss across the space that no longer seemed so immense. "Why don't you go and order us a pizza or some Chinese food. My credit card is in my purse. Oh, and before you go, could you put that CD on again for me? What's the name of that band anyway?"

"Nomeansno."
"How odd. And the one before that?"
"Metallica."
"Aren't they lovely?"

WTF?

The world is full of surprises.

Twenty-nine

When Bryan entered his bedroom, he found Jessie sitting cross-legged on his bed.

Three weeks had passed since he and his mother had finished sorting through Michelle's stuff. They'd turned her bedroom into a sort of second-floor den. They painted it a soft green, put up bookshelves, installed a flat-screen television and a stereo. They tore up the carpet, polished the wood floor underneath and covered it with a blue-and-gold Persian rug his mother had bought a few years ago at a garage sale. They added a second-hand couch and two overstuffed chairs. The room felt warm and inviting, and Bryan spent a great deal of his spare time there, reading or playing guitar or listening to music.

He'd been at Dr. Spahic's that afternoon. When he got home, Stella had just finished cleaning the kitchen. She greeted him cheerfully. "There's someone upstairs waiting to see you," she said.

"Who?"

"Why don't you go on up and see for yourself." She handed him a large piece of banana bread. "Fresh today," she said and smiled.

He bound up the staircase, curious about the mysterious visitor, and discovered Jessie slouched on his bed, chin in her hands, her dark hair falling over her shoulders.

"Hey," she greeted him. "I was about to give up on you ever showing up." She locked eyes with him, daring him to send her away.

"Jessie?" He resisted the urge to rub his eyes, to pinch himself. "I . . . I . . . uh . . . I guess I didn't expect you. But I'm glad you're here," he tacked on quickly, afraid she might misunderstand— might disappear.

"You can come in, you know—that is, unless you need to hold up the doorway." She winked at him. "Kidding, but come on in. I don't bite."

God, I'm such an idiot. He tried not to imagine what he must look like to her, stuck in the door like a praying mantis, wide-eyed, tall, skinny and a new zit blooming on his nose, unsure whether to bolt or enter the room, his room! "I guess I'm surprised. Stella didn't say it was . . . that you were here."

"I asked her not to. I've missed her banana bread, as much as I've missed her. And you," she added. "I thought maybe if you knew I was here, you'd bolt."

"You were right about that."

Wrong thing to say.

"I don't mean it like that." He took a tentative step toward her. "I'm glad you're here . . . at least I'm not gonna run. Actually, I have no idea what I'm feeling. Not anger. Fear?"

Shut up! Shut up! You sound like a maniac or an idiot.

"Dr. Spahic has a word for it: 'alexithymia.' It's a condition where a person can't describe how they are feeling in words. I looked it up online. The website said it's like *the words are present but the melody is missing.* Shit." He smiled sheepishly. "I guess I'll shut up now."

Jessie snorted. She folded herself in half and laughed until tears flowed down her cheeks. Bryan folded his arms and tried to look hurt, but in the end, he joined in, and the tension between them melted. By the time they'd wiped away their tears, Bryan had planted himself on the opposite end of the bed, facing Jessie.

"Seriously," he said, but without rancour, "What's going on, Jess? What are you doing here, besides eating banana bread and laughing at me?"

"Like I said, I missed you. You didn't seem to be too interested in talking to me, so I called your mom, and we had a long talk— about you. I hope you don't mind, but I needed to know what was up. She explained to me about . . . stuff."

"Stuff? What stuff?" Bryan knew, but he wanted to make sure.

"She told me about the endorphins. You know. The cutting. I thought when you showed me the burns on your arms that it was a one-off. I mean, I guess I should have guessed about the cutting, but it wouldn't have occurred to me that you'd do that . . . I mean, it shocked me. I couldn't figure out why you'd . . . well, I guess I didn't want to believe it."

"Oh, shit. So now you know the whole truth. Did the two of you figure out what makes the loony tick? What motivates the freak?" He heard, but couldn't control, the self-pity in his voice. *What can she possibly see in me?*

"Whatever. Interpret it any way you want. God, you can be such a jerk. I didn't come here to fight with you. Okay?"

Bryan shook his head, totally deflated. "Whatever."

"Anyway, I can think of another way to release endorphins. If you're up to it."

Is she coming on to me?

"Really. Do you mean you want to . . . what about *What's-his-face?*"

"No, silly. I mean exercise. I thought we could go for a walk." Jessie chuckled. "Come on, Bryan. Stella is downstairs. And besides, What's-his-face is Brad, and he's still in my life."

"Still hanging on, huh?"

"He's okay." She shrugged. "I don't mind him. He's nice to me."

"That sounds like true love to me," Bryan said, feeling instantly better.

She stood. "Another topic for another day. Come on. Let's go for that walk."

Argument would be futile. "Okay. But I'd rather listen to music," he protested, following her into the hallway.

As they passed Michelle's old room, she said, "I like it a lot. It rocks."

She's been snooping. "Me, too."

Stella had finished for the day, and she and his mother were talking quietly in the living room. They both beamed at Bryan and Jessie as they headed out. "Have fun," his mother said, as if he did this kind of thing everyday.

"Sure, Mom." He grinned at Jessie. "I'm not usually allowed out without the third degree," he explained to her, once out of earshot of his mom and Stella. He hoped she couldn't detect how nervous and unsure he felt being with her. He hoped agreeing to this walk wouldn't turn out to be a grave mistake.

"This has been hard on her, and on Stella." Jessie squeezed his arm. "On all of you."

"I guess."

"Your mom trusts me," says Jessie. "And she loves you. I really like her."

"She's all right. Better with Dad out of the picture. Although who knows how long that will last."

"Yeah, your dad. What a piece of work he is."

Bryan couldn't hold back the laughter. So others saw it, too.

"You've always been honest, Jess."

She smiled and took him by the arm. They moved off down the sidewalk in easy silence, as if two years and more hadn't passed, as if the whole world hadn't spun on its axis since the last time they were together, as if Bryan wasn't wacko.

Eventually they got around to talking about school and university and people they knew in common. Jessie told him about the trip to Paris she'd taken with her French class in the spring and about her mom's new store. She talked about the new music she'd discovered, and movies she'd seen, both good and bad. Bryan mostly listened, and the time flew by. She talked freely, unperturbed by his extended, but easy, silence.

"You want to do this again tomorrow?" she asked. They'd strolled for over an hour, arriving back at Bryan's house just as dusk settled in. Mom had turned on the porch light, and the house seemed inviting in a way that Bryan had never noticed before.

"I used to dread coming home," he said. "I used to brace myself to face Dad and all his BS." Bryan was stalling and he knew it. He could walk and talk with her forever.

"I know," she said. "Like I said before, your dad is a real piece of work. So what do you think about doing this again tomorrow?"

"I guess so. I mean it's not like I'm a big walker or anything, but yeah. Unless, of course, it's gonna upset *What's-his-face*," he scoffed, his eyes sparkling.

"Very funny. And it's Brad."

"Right. Do you want to come in?"

"No. I've got stuff I need to work on. I've got a paper due, but I'll see you around four tomorrow." She dashed across the street and climbed into a blue sports car.

"Hey," Bryan yelled. "I didn't know you drove, let alone owned a car."

"It's my parents' car. They traded in the old one. I got my license while you were in the hospital. My parents said I could drive as soon as I turned seventeen, but I wasn't really into it, until this year. Anyway, I did tell you, but you forgot." She stuck out her tongue out at him. "See you later." A quick wave and she was gone. The whole street—and Bryan—felt empty.

"Damn, I forgot all about that," Bryan mouthed to her departing car.

Maybe Dr. Spahic had a point. Maybe I am self-centered sometimes. I can make it up to her.

Minutes later, he still stood staring at the space where her parked car had been. He didn't notice his mom peeking out through the living room window at him. She smiled, seeing the loopy half-grin on his face. "Thank you, God," she whispered, crossing her fingers. "Let it last."

"Did you have a good time with Jessie?" His mom kept her voice neutral, but Bryan sensed her excitement.

"I had a great time," he said, mostly to set her at ease and stop her questions, but as the words spilled out of him, he knew they were true.

That night, after dinner, he typed in his journal:

I did something with someone else today. I went for a walk with Jessie. We didn't talk about anything really, nothing earth-shattering, but I can't remember having a better time.

It became Jessie and Bryan's habit to walk together every afternoon. Bryan looked forward to it all day, and at night he fell asleep replaying everything they had said to each other. Their conversations varied from silly to serious, but the one thing that they really needed to discuss lay like a wall between them. Every day it grew a little higher.

Jessie took her time.

Thirty

It was around this time that Bryan's dad started to wage a verbal war with his mom. He called daily, at random times, and if nobody answered the phone, he'd keep calling until he either got someone on the other end, or he gave up. On Stella's cleaning days, she'd pick up. "Nobody's home," she'd lie, "but I'll tell them you called."

Of course he knew it wasn't true, but there was little he could do about it. Bryan's mother wouldn't answer the phone at all, and Bryan had never bothered to before, but that had changed now that he and Jessie had renewed their friendship. If only Jessie would leave messages. "I hate talking to machines," she'd confessed. One day he would tell her about his father, but he wasn't ready to yet. For him, the truth was too painful.

The phone had been ringing relentlessly for the last hour. Bryan ignored it for as long as he could—he put on headphones and cranked up the volume—but in the end, fear of missing Jessie's call won out over caution, and the next time it rang, he picked it up, not bothering to even check the caller ID—his fingers crossed that it would be her.

"Hello?"

"Hello, Bryan."

Dad. He'd talked to his father a couple of times since being released from the hospital, but he'd found the conversations difficult—worse because his parents hadn't really separated, but it was obvious to anyone who wanted to see it that his father would never live with them again.

"Bryan. I know you're there. I can hear you breathing. You've been a mouth-breather since you were a baby." Even from such a distance, Bryan reacted as he would if his father were in the next room. He heard the scorn in his father's voice, disguised by a snigger, and his heart began to race. All the edges of his world began to close in on him. His hands, clutching the receiver, were cold and clammy.

"Hey, Dad." He swallowed hard twice. "I'm here."
"A 'Hello' would be nice. Speak up. I can hardly hear you. Hello? I guess we have a bad connection."

"Yes. I'd agree with you on that one." Bryan knew the irony had escaped his dad, or if it hadn't, he let it go.

"You don't sound too happy to talk to me. Have you been listening to your mother?"

"Mom doesn't talk about you."
"That's just great. How is your mom?"
"Why don't you ask her yourself?"

"I would if she would speak to me." When Bryan didn't reply, his father continued. "I'll bet she's turned you against me, too. I'm the innocent one, yet I get all the blame. It's bloody unfair," he whined.

First the self-pity, then the abuse. "You don't have to talk to him if you don't want to," Dr. Spahic had advised.

"I have to go, Dad," he gulped. "Bye."

"Don't you dare hang up on me, you little . . ."

Bryan hit the OFF button and slumped down onto the sofa. The headache didn't creep up on him; it arrived like a logging truck, screeching into his consciousness. *Shit.* He pulled himself up, stumbled to the liquor cabinet and poured himself a full glass of vodka.

Later, when his mother came home, he didn't tell her about the phone call. She'd discover the missing vodka on her own.

"Sometimes, I just know my emotions will kill me. I'll choke to death on feeling. Especially when I'm angry. Rage, that's what I felt talking to Dad." Bryan was comfortable in Dr. Spahic's office, slouched in a big chair, his feet propped on the ottoman. "I swallow those feelings, and next thing you know, there's a monster sitting in the pit of my stomach. It makes me feel physically sick."

"So how do you get rid of the monster?"

"How do I do it?" Bryan closed his eyes. "I soothe it—a drink or two and when that doesn't work, I do a little self-surgery. Or at least I used to."

"And now?"

"I still think about the perfect cut, and I've been known to sneak a drink, but most of the time, I go play guitar, or I write in my journal—songs, poetry . . . When I'm with Jessie, though, I never feel that way."

"What way? Try to put it into words, Bryan."

"Claustrophobic. Like I'm trying to claw my way of a narrow, black hole in the sand, but I can't. The more I dig, the more the sand falls down into my mouth, my eyes, my ears. I won't make it to the surface."

"Uh-huh. You've really identified this sense of hopelessness you have well. Now try to tell me what you feel like when you're with Jessie?"

"Good. She sees the hole and she steers me around it. She listens and she tells me stuff and we laugh."

"That is friendship. Does anyone else make you feel that way?"

"My mom a bit, now that Dad is gone. You, in a way, but that's your job." He grinned. "I feel that way when I'm listening to music or playing guitar."

"Do you have any idea or can you be more specific about what you're feeling when you say, 'I feel that way when I'm listening to music or playing guitar?' Can you try to put a name to that emotion?"

"I don't know." He thinks about it. "Not dead."

"That's a start. Think about it and we'll talk more about it next time. Do you have any idea who brings out the monster in you?"

"Stupid people—like the kids at my old school, some teachers, my dad, for sure." Bryan leaned back in his chair. Even thinking about his father sucked the energy out of him.

"Hating people takes a lot of energy, wastes a lot of time," said Dr. Spahic. "Do you think it's worth it?"

"I don't know another way."

Bryan was holding the razor in his hand when Jessie burst into the bathroom. She had always been that way—exuberant—a summer storm, filled with light and energy. He welcomed it ninety-nine percent of the time, but in this moment it only irritated him. He'd been as cantankerous as a bee-stung bear since his father's phone call. He dropped the razor into the sink and swore.

"God, what are you doing?" she shrieked, covering her mouth with her hand.

He hadn't any intention of slicing himself, but only an idiot would believe that, and Jessie was no fool. "It's not what you think," he attempted, but it sounded lame, even to him. "Look." He rolled up his sleeves and held out his arms to let her see his scars. She grimaced. "Scars—train tracks, but no fresh cuts. See for yourself." He rolled his sleeves back down, totally deflated. "I know what you're thinking. Why should you believe me? Most people wouldn't."

"You *don't* know what I'm thinking," she snapped. He tried to gauge what she was feeling and saw curiosity, maybe irritation, but not disgust, reflected in her expression. "Why can't you just trust me for once? Tell me what upset you."

"All right." To buy a little time, he trudged from the bathroom to his bedroom, and she trailed after him. He took the neatly folded pieces of tissue from his sock drawer and tossed them in the garbage. Then he went to his window, glanced at the dull winter light and heaved a sigh. "Sometimes I hold the razor in my hand to convince myself that I can say no."

Jessie put her hands on her hips and looked at him candidly. "Maybe . . . who knows, but just maybe . . . you'll feel better if you talk about it."

"Dad called. He's been calling a lot lately. We don't want to talk to him. He and Mom fight, and most of the time she ends up in tears. I haven't talked to him in months. Anyway, I answered the phone in case . . . well, I thought it might be you. You never leave a message. I didn't want to miss your call," he added abruptly.

"I am so sorry. I had no idea. If you'd told me, I would have left messages." She approached him slowly, as if she thought he'd push her away. When he didn't, she wrapped her arms around his waist. "It's okay to cry." Her voice was muffled against his chest. He hadn't realized he'd been crying. "Bryan, it's time for you to tell the truth to both your mom and dad. I'll help you."

"I don't know if I have the words. I don't know where to begin."

"Write it. Write a letter to your mom. You said the writing comes easily to you. She can show it to your dad if she wants. I'll read it over before you give it to her. Bryan, I know some of the truth and I'm still with you. It'll make you feel better, take a huge load off you." She waited until she felt the shaking in his body subside. "It's not your fault, you know."

"You don't know everything, Jessie."

"What I don't know, I can guess." She let go of him and led him gently to his bed, where she sat him down. "I know where to start." She retrieved Michelle's Rosa Hurricane from where it had sat untouched since his mother had asked him to take it. "It's something to do with this, isn't it?"

He nodded. Blew his nose. "Yeah. I'll need a screwdriver."

"I'll get you one." She got up, kissed him on the top of the head and went in search of the tool he needed without asking any questions. While she was gone, he held the guitar on his lap, caressing the soft blonde wood, no longer fighting the memories. In a weird way, the Rosa Hurricane was Michelle. He plucked at the strings—even out of tune, the beautiful sound evoked strong memories of Michelle, giving him the courage to do what he had to do next.

When Jessie returned, she handed him the screwdriver. "She sure could make music," she said. "I remember you told me Michelle said something about her guitar the night of the accident. You told me before the ambulance took you away."

"I did?"

"You did."

"Oh. Well, Michelle said: 'I don't want to get into this in any kind of detail, but in the event of something ever happening to me, I've left a note.' She said it was in the back of her guitar."

Bryan took the screwdriver from Jessie. "I can't do it." He handed her back the screwdriver along with the guitar.

He watched nervously as she turned the Rosa over and took out the four screws in the back, one by one. She carefully removed the silver plate and handed the guitar to him. "You have to do this part."

Inside the shallow cavity, tucked away as he knew it would be, was a piece of folded, plain, white paper. Across the front, scrawled in uneven, choppy handwriting was his name. *Bryan*. He recognized Michelle's handwriting and felt himself falling back into that dark place. He felt Jesse's comforting hand on his back and inhaled deeply. *I can do this*. For over two years, he'd known the letter would be there, but looking at it in its physical form was somehow unnerving. He stared at it for a few minutes, then placed the guitar gently on the bed. His hands were shaking, but he felt calm inside. "So, you've known all this time?"

Jessie nodded. "Remember, I was with you both that night."

"And you've never said a thing to anyone?"

"It was always up to you, Bry. I was just there." She wasn't apologizing, only stating the truth.

Bryan knew he didn't have to explain to her. He knew she would not press him. "Thanks."

Thirty-one

Dear Mom,

You said to me that there are things a mother should never have to tell a son. You were right. There are also things a son should never have to tell a mother, but I have to tell you this. I have to, so I can save myself and maybe what is left of our family. If you can't forgive me after reading this, so be it.

Rest assured, I have not forgiven myself.

It might come as a big surprise to you to know that Michelle wasn't perfect. Dad thought she was, or at least that's how it seemed to me, and maybe that caused a lot of problems.

Michelle protected me. We talked about that. In a way she protected us both. She did this by standing up to Dad—something I'm only just learning to do. She did this by deflecting his criticisms, and by keeping a sense of humour and sense of fun. All of those actions took their toll on her, though. She hated the way Dad treated us. She hated the taunting and baiting and sarcasm, the rules, the shoulds and should-nots, the stony silences that went on for days, the control.

But the thing that really bothered her was being the chosen one, the most-loved, and the best-treated. I know, because she told me this. She thought I was weak because I always did what I was told, but she never understood that I was afraid, or if she did, maybe she just hoped to make me strong.

You remember that when we were little kids, Dad believed in 'spare the rod, spoil the child'—one of his favourite and most overused expressions? I never understood why you always pretended not to know, until Michelle told me that all of your 'accidents' were not accidents at all, just more of Dad's 'discipline.'

Somehow, she always knew what was going on.

I used to hate you because you never protected me.

Michelle told me why, but I still couldn't stop blaming you.

Michelle dealt with this in her own way. She cut herself, and I watched sometimes, and sometimes, but not often, I did it, too. She said, "At least this way you can be in control of who hurts you." It made sense.

Dad caught Michelle one day. We were both in her room and we thought we had the house to ourselves. Michelle always turned the music up really loud if nobody was home, but Dad arrived home earlier than she'd expected. I was only about eleven, so Michelle was already fifteen. If she hadn't had the music on full blast, we would have heard Dad calling, and we would have heard him climbing the stairs to look for us.

We didn't hear a thing until her door flew open and Dad towered over us. He'd come up to tell us to keep the noise down, but when he saw what Michelle was doing to her arm, he went nuts.

For once, it wasn't my entire fault. Still, he sent a few kicks my way and of course that set Michelle off. She lost it—flung herself at him. Of course Dad was bigger and stronger and crazier—he let Michelle have it—but he didn't hit her in places that anyone would ever see.

Remember? She pretended to be sick for about a week.

Dad threatened both of us—scared us out of telling you what had happened—scared us into a silence that has lasted all of these years.

Even so, Dad never touched Michelle again. You see, she'd had enough. I don't know what she said to Dad, but he never laid a finger on her again. He never entered her room after that. Instead he treated her like a princess— she could do whatever she wanted—no repercussions. Suddenly, I was the target of all of his hate.

After that, she cut more. She changed. Around you and Dad, she kept up an act, but I saw her become aloof, bitter, cynical, and she started drinking—not at parties and stuff, she didn't go out much—but on her own. Mom, I know this is hard for you to hear, but it's time for the truth. Michelle could hide her depression, but I couldn't, so I looked like the weird one.

Dad and you concentrated on me. Michelle barely got noticed. I didn't know what to do. I just got to hate myself more and more. You can see why, Mom.

She started talking about death all the time. "One of these days, I'm going to kill myself," she would say. "That

will teach Dad." I never took her seriously, even though
she started to hurt herself more and more, and they weren't
always surface wounds.

I didn't know what to do. I didn't know who to tell.

No one else knew except for me how sick she was. And I
never told. She made me promise to keep her secret, and
I did, and I have, right up until now. I think Dad guessed
that I knew more than I let on and that was one of the
reasons why he blamed me when she died. He's right; I am
a coward. I should have said something to somebody, but
who? You? You never wanted to hear the truth. After all,
it had been right in front of your eyes for all of those years
when we were growing up.

That night, the night she died, I'd known for a while that
Michelle didn't plan to live a long life. For some reason,
my intuition told me to get out of the house; something
about her mood that day made me think she'd hit the
wall. I didn't even have the guts to be with my only sister
when she was planning to take her own life.

I was so angry with her. Angry and scared. And half-
convinced that she wouldn't leave me. But she'd told
me earlier in the day that she'd had enough. She'd been
in a big fight with Dad—he was still treating her like a

little kid—and he threatened to take away her guitar. That guitar meant the world to Michelle. Not everyone understood what it meant to her, but the guitar became alive in her hands and music was her world. This time, Dad really meant it, and she couldn't take it.

Jessie came over—we were going to the party together. Before we left, Michelle called me into her room. I remember she looked so tired and grey that night. I remember exactly what she said, "If anything ever happens to me, I've left something in the back of my guitar. It's up to you to find it in the event of... In case something happens to me."

"What is it?" I asked.

"A note," she said.

I knew what she meant. She'd always been drawn to the dark side—she loved singing about it, and most of the music she liked was pretty bleak. I should have stuck around and talked to her, but I had a date with Jessie, and in reality, I didn't want to know. I really blew it. Maybe I could have stopped her if I'd shown a little more interest?

(I don't blame you for hating me, Mom.)

I went to the party. Jessie and I had a big fight. You see, I couldn't get Michelle off my mind. I called her at home, and she'd already been drinking and smoking pot, and she sounded pretty wrecked. That in itself wasn't out of character although she'd always found it stupidly easy to hide that from you, and I think she knew that nobody really noticed her. I think that hurt.

"This is the night, man," were her exact words. "I'm going to miss you, little brother, but I can't do this anymore." She hung up.

I panicked. I knew I had to get to her before she killed herself, so I called you and made up the story about not having a bus pass, not having any money and needing a ride home. I told you some story about there being trouble brewing at the party and I was afraid, so you sent Michelle over to get me.

You see, Mom, I thought if I could talk to her, I could save her. I thought I meant that much to her.

Jessie knew what was going down—not everything, but she had an idea. She got really mad at me and told me I needed to call someone who had some experience dealing with kids who are suicidal. She didn't know about the cutting or about how bad it was for us at home, but she knew Michelle was in trouble, and that I was in over my head. I wouldn't listen to her. We had another fight—a huge fight—and she said, "If something happens to her, you won't be able to live with this decision."

God, how right she was.

When I called home that night, you wanted me to take a cab, I remember that, but then Dad got on the phone and when I told him the same story he got into that 'a family should be loyal to its members' speech, just like I knew he would. He insisted that Michelle come and get me. She was so pissed off. Dad took Michelle's guitar and said he would return it when her marks improved, when she stopped mouthing off and a whole list of other demands.

Michelle gave in easily—that should have been a warning. Normally Michelle would kill for that guitar, and normally Dad wouldn't talk to her like that. He must have sensed her vulnerability. I don't know what you remember about that night, Mom, but Michelle told me that she'd said goodbye to you, but you wouldn't realize it until you gave it some thought. Remember that day a little while ago when we were going through her stuff and you said to me, "Sometimes I think Michelle chose to leave." I knew that you were thinking about that night and her goodbye.

She told me that when she handed the guitar over to Dad,

she said to him, "You win, you bastard," and ran out the door, leaving Dad standing there open-mouthed. I'll bet you anything Dad never told you that . . .

"And this is what I've put down so far. I printed it out for you." Bryan handed Jessie the letter, hoping he was doing the right thing by placing so much trust in her.

"Are you going to stare at me the whole time I'm reading?" She frowned. "Because if you are, I'm going to lock myself in the bathroom, so I can concentrate."

"Sorry. This is way harder than I thought it would be."

"You're a great writer."

"I didn't mean the writing. I meant sharing it with you."

While she read, Bryan paced the perimeter of his room, never taking his eyes off her face, trying to gauge her reaction through her expression. About halfway through, she paused and looked up at him. "Oh, my God, Bryan. I never knew it was so bad."

"Nobody did."

"I'm so sorry about what I said," she mumbled, her eyes filling with tears.

"Don't be. You were right."

"It's all coming back so vividly. The pieces all fit together." Jessie could no longer hold back the tears. Bryan sat down beside her and drew her close to him. He held her until she calmed down, and then, wishing there was no Brad, wishing it could be different, he forced himself to let her go. "There's something I want to play for you. Remember this song? It was the last song Michelle ever played."

Thirty-two

The music, an audio time machine, transported them back to that night, back to the few hours before and after the terrible crash. Bryan closed his eyes and let the memories in:

Michelle is sitting on the couch. Her head is bent over the guitar, and her fingers move deftly up and down the neck, while her body sways in time to the melody and her foot taps out the beat. Every so often, she pauses, for a drag of her smoke or a mouthful of beer. It is very late and most of the kids have left the party; those remaining have stayed so that they can hear her play. Bryan has long given up on trying to convince Michelle to leave. He knows that once the music takes over, there is little he can do but wait until she is ready to go. Usually this is not a problem. But tonight, *Bryan thinks*, nothing is as it seems.

As if reading his mind, Michelle glances up, and her eyes search the room until she finds him. She nods, a motion so subtle as to be imperceptible to the other people in the room. Her dark eyes are glassy but beneath the film of alcohol-induced tranquility, Bryan sees a world of hurt. He raises his beer bottle to her. "Cheers," he mouths and is rewarded by a smile.

She continues to play. Her body is angled toward Bryan, and she seems to be singing directly to him. Bryan feels as if they are the only two people in the room.

Except that Jessie stands framed by the doorway, her arms crossed, her shoulders tight and braced for a fight. Bryan wishes she would stop glaring at him. He turns his back to her and immerses himself in the music. She's making magic, not music, he thinks.

When the song is finished, someone yells, "More!" Others join in.

Michelle shrugs, but Bryan can tell she is pleased. "One more . . ." she agrees, " . . . and then it's over." Something about the way she says it makes the hair on Bryan's neck stand to attention.

She throws everything she's got into the next tune, pounding on the guitar until she breaks a string. "Damn it," she grins sheepishly at the guitar's owner. "Sorry, man."

"No worries," he gives her the thumbs-up. "Just do me a favour and give us one more tune."

"Can't say no to that, can I? But then I'm done." Michelle sits for a moment and then, in spite of the broken string, begins to play for the last time.

It is a song Bryan knows well: Death Cab for Cutie's "I Will Follow You Into the Dark."

When she arrives at the last verse, he realizes that tonight everything is going to change forever. Even then, it's too late to change the outcome.

Her voice quavers on the last line of the last verse of the last song. Once finished, she puts down the guitar that does not belong to her, but has never sounded so beautiful. A beer is pressed into her calloused hand, followed by another and then another. Bryan watches furtively. She is pretty loaded when Bryan approaches her again. "We've got to go. We don't have to go home, but let's get out of here." At least if he can get her out the door, it's a start.

"I'm not ready yet, dude." Michelle's words roll over each other and turn into one continuous, incompressible sentence, "A couple more beer, and I'll be gone. I promise."

"This is stupid. Why are you so afraid of leaving?" He is goading her.

"Leave her alone." Some guy pushes Bryan aside. "Let her play guitar." He is very drunk as well.

"No. No more guitar," Michelle says firmly, unwrapping the guy's arm from her waist. "I've played my last song." Words that still haunt Bryan.

Finally, Michelle decides she is ready to leave. It is an hour later when they put on their coats. Jessie has already gone, furious, and as they approach the car, her parting words to Bryan ring in his mind: "You'd better not get in a car with Michelle when she's like this. If she doesn't kill you both, she'll kill someone else."

"Take it easy, Jessie," Bryan had retorted. "We're fine. Why don't you go worry about somebody else for a change? You're not my mother, you know." Bryan knows he is being unreasonable and immature, but nobody is allowed to get between Bryan and his sister. Not even Jessie.

Hurt, she'd stomped away. Knowing she is right makes him angry. "Screw you," he mouthed to her departing back.

All of this comes back to him as they leave the party. Outside, the street that was jammed with cars is now nearly empty. Michelle's car is halfway down the block. The moon hides between dark storm clouds, and Bryan does up his jacket and squints at Michelle. "Freezing out here." If she hears him, she doesn't acknowledge it.

Even though Bryan is having trouble walking a straight line, he supports Michelle, who is completely trashed and stumbling. Once at the car, Bryan hesitates before opening the door. I'm going to wake up to a world of hurt, *he thinks.*

The car is already idling when he climbs in beside Michelle, but they do not pull away from the curb. She grips the steering wheel, but still she doesn't pull away from the curb. Bryan waves his hand in front of her frozen face, but she will not be distracted. He feels increasingly nervous. "Maybe we should walk home."

When Michelle finally speaks, her voice is faraway, dreamy. "Okay, Little Bro. Listen up. I don't want to get into this in any kind of detail, but in the event of something ever happening to me, I've left a note."

"A note?"

"Yeah. Like a letter. A note. I've stashed it behind the plate in my guitar. It's got your name on it."

"Why, in case I mix it up with some other note that I happen to find in some random guitar?"

"Funny! Now listen, I'm serious. I know you made a promise to me a long time ago, but if for some reason I'm not around, you can break it or keep it or whatever. It won't matter one way or the other to me—not where I'm going."

"What's that supposed to mean? You wouldn't take off and leave me alone in that house? I don't believe you. This is BS, man."

Bryan watches her shoulders droop, and then he thinks he's won. He'll ask her what's up, and when she tells him, he'll make her take him with her. But just to make sure, he adds, "I don't want to be left behind," knowing how much he sounds like a snivelling baby.

"I told you, no details." Michelle shifts the car into drive. "Besides," she adds, her voice kinder, "you don't wanna come with me, not to this place." Moving out into the road, she forgets to check in the mirror and over her shoulder. They are on a quiet side street that turns onto a main road at the end of the block. She drives slowly, narrowly missing several parked cars.

"Take it easy," mutters Bryan. "I'm getting out if you sideswipe a car. Dad will kill you."

That makes Michelle laugh. "There should always be a backup plan," she sniggers, and then suddenly she is serious again. "I can't take you with me. There's only room for one on this trip. Besides, there are some things a girl just has to do alone." She squeezes Bryan's shoulder. "But if I could take anyone, it would be you." Bryan pushes her hand away. He's mad at her, but he's also feeling confused. Scared, too.

"You're going to have to look out for Mom. She's helpless against that bastard." Michelle's voice fractures when she says 'Mom.' He looks at her, and finally he gets it. Her profile is determined, her cheeks wet, her breathing steady, but forced.

"Are you out of your mind?" he yells. They've reached the end of the side street. "I'm not going to leave you alone, not for a second."

Michelle turns to him, her eyes black with fury. "Shut up. I'm tired of everything—of people bossing me around, of people depending on me, of . . ." She fights for control. ". . . And I'm mostly tired of being me," she whispers, pulling out onto the main road that will take them home.

"I heard the sound of metal on metal," Jessie interjected. "I was going back to find you. I had such a weird feeling—like something bad was going to happen to you."

Bryan jumped. He had forgotten Jessie was beside him. He had forgotten that he had asked her to listen to his story.

"I heard screaming, too. I felt sick, but it didn't surprise me at all. It was as if she was headed that way all along, and all of us were a part of it. None of us did a thing about it." She took his hand. Bryan was grateful. "It wasn't just you. I think we all knew."

"For a long time after it happened, I didn't remember a thing.
Now I remember everything, except for how to feel."

Thirty-three

It took a lot of guts combined with encouragement from Jessie for Bryan to agree to hand the letter over to his mom. "Shouldn't I wait until Stella is here, in case Mom gets totally upset?"

Jessie thought it over. "I don't think so. It's up to her to decide who she wants to share it with. Anyway, that's a delaying tactic, and I think you should get it over with immediately, before you change your mind."

"Yeah. Okay. I guess." He'd spent the last fifteen minutes pacing the length of his room, sure that the walls were closing in on him, chock full of anxiety about how his mother would react. After all, she'd gone through so much, did she really need this and could she handle it? He had to trust Jessie—*she's never let me down before*, he reasoned, coming to a decision. "All right, but let's get it over with before I change my mind." He smiled weakly at her.

"Trust me," she said, taking him firmly by the arm and leading him downstairs. "It's the right thing to do."

They found his mother in the kitchen fussing over her house-plants. As soon as she saw Jessie, her face lit up. Since Michelle's death, Bryan had cut himself off from the world, and it had taken him over two years to begin to step gingerly back into the land of the living. Isabelle had witnessed the change in her son's behaviour since he'd reconnected with Jessie. She'd somehow gained his trust and friendship. Isabelle appreciated that while Bryan had come a long way since being released from the hospital, he still lay at risk of skidding back into that dark place—a realization that terrified her more than anything.

"Hi, guys," she said, blowing a kiss at both of them. She wore her hair in a ponytail, and a streak of soil ran down her cheek. "I repotted this plant a week ago, and it hasn't done well since. I suppose I should have left it in its old soil." She pulled off her gardening gloves and chucked them into the sink. "What about a pot of tea? I could use a break and some company."

"I'd love one," enthused Jessie, before Bryan could refuse. He stood beside her mutely. She elbowed him in the ribs. "Tell her," she mouthed, "and stop gaping."

Bryan gawked at her, his forehead creased. Couldn't she see he wanted to speak, but the words were frozen on his lips? "I can't," he mouthed back.

"What are you two up to? If there's a secret, I want in on it. Here, Bryan." His mother handed him three mugs. "Put these on the table. Jess, can you get the milk and sugar?"

"Absolutely." While she searched through the cupboards for the sugar bowl, Jessie casually said, "Actually, this is perfect. There's something Bryan wants to show you. What better time than over a cup of tea?"

"This sounds intriguing. Can you tell me a bit more, Bryan?"

The kettle whistled, and Bryan breathed an inward sigh of relief, thankful for the minutes gained while his mom busied herself with the tea. She placed the pot on the table with a plate of chocolate chip cookies. "Courtesy of Stella," she said, offering the plate to Jessie with a smile. "So?" His mother leaned forward, elbows on the table, eyes on Bryan. "What is it you want to show me?"

Bryan cleared his throat. "It's uh . . . here." He rested his eyes on her, and then looked away nervously. "Here," he handed the note across the table. "I wrote this for you."

As his mother unfolded the paper, Bryan sensed that Jessie was nervous, too. She twirled her red hair in restless fingers, cleared her throat, and tapped her leg incessantly on the floor. Her green eyes didn't keep still for a second, darting around the room as if looking for a way to escape.

Bryan distracted himself by studying Jessie, unable to look at his mom while she was reading. Jesse could, though—stealing peeks out of the corner of her eyes. When his mother had read through the letter once, she went over it again—this time, more slowly. Once finished, she covered her mouth with her hand and blinked back tears. "Was it . . . was it a suicide note she left for you? Are you telling me she was planning to . . . to kill herself all along?"

Bryan nodded mutely. "Not that night," Jessie clarified. "That night was an accident—but she planned the outcome and it came early."

"She addressed it only to you, honey?"
"Yeah."
"You poor thing. May I see it?"

Bryan had expected she'd want to see it, so at Jessie's suggestion, he'd brought it downstairs. He fumbled in his pocket until he found it, and then he passed it to her clumsily. He waited for his mom's wrath, but when their fingers touched, she looked at him, not with hate, but with sadness, and love.

"Go on, Mom, read it."

She nodded and moved her chair closer to Bryan, and taking his hand, gripped it in her own.

Jessie, seeing this, knew she and Bryan had done the right thing. She put a box of tissues on the table in front of Bryan, then pushed back her chair. "I'll call you later," she said, backing out of the room, but they were too engrossed in the note and in each other to notice her exit.

Bryan,

Little Bro, if you are reading this, it means that I have finally achieved my goal. Please don't cry—I'm where I want to be—I don't believe in an afterlife. I don't believe there is a God, but I believe that by breaking my connection with the physical world, I will merge with the earth and the sky, freeing me from the imprisonment of my body.

I haven't decided how or when, but I want you to know that there are no accidents. The world is a shitty place and I don't feel anything anymore. Except really bad about leaving you. My Rosa Hurricane is yours. I don't care about anything else. I'll try not to leave a mess.

*I guess you want reasons. I can't explain it all but I'll give
you something. I hate myself. I hate myself for dragging
you down with me. I hate myself for asking you to keep a
promise when I know secrets are the worst things. I should
have never got you into hurting yourself.*

*I guess I'm a coward. I know you. Dad will find some way
to make you responsible for my death—and you'll just
go along with it. I've come to realize that nothing is as it
seems. You have covered for me, protected me, but not vice
versa. I'm sorry. One piece of advice: stand up for yourself,
especially to Dad.*

Tell Mom I'm sorry. And that I love you both.
Michelle

When she had finished reading the note, Mom folded it as Michelle
had, leaving only his name visible. She pushed it into his hands.
"Thank you," she said, and pressed her hand against his cheek. "We
have a lot of healing to do."

That night Bryan sat up late and played the guitar that Michelle
had wanted him to have.

He feels.

Epilogue

Dr. Spahic saw the difference in him right away. Her eyes crinkled as he lifted Poppins off the overstuffed chair and rearranged the purring cat on his knee. For a moment neither doctor nor patient said a word. It was Bryan who broke the silence. "Something's happened," he said.

"Can you put it into words?"

Bryan grinned. "No. No, I can't do that..." He rose and Poppins glared at him. "Sorry, kitty. This will just take a second." He went over to where Dr. Spahic stood and wrapped his arms around her in a bear hug. "Thank you," he said. "Thank you for believing in me and for showing me that I'm not such a bad guy, after all."

Not cutting, putting an end to it, wouldn't be the easiest thing in the world. He knew that, and he knew he couldn't do it on his own, so in the end he turned to his therapist and to his mom and to his best friend, Jessie. In his weaker moments, he didn't believe that they would stick with him, but they did. Finally the day came when he put the razor away for good. He even stopped drinking. He worried that he would spend the rest of his days answering a lot of questions. He prepared the appropriate answers. Often when he wore short-sleeved shirts, someone might look at him sideways, but they never said much. They didn't care.

Nobody does.

CUT

Except maybe a few people.

The ones who count.

Historical References:

496–406 BCE

Sophocles, Ancient Greece

In Sophocles' play, *Oedipus the King*, Oedipus unwittingly kills his father and marries his mother, Jocasta. After Jocasta kills herself, Oedipus blinds himself by sticking her golden brooches through his eyes while crying, "Wicked, wicked eyes! You shall not see me nor my shame. Not see my present crime. Go dark, for all time blind, to what you should have never seen."

460–370 BCE

Hippocrates

Hippocrates' theory of the four humours governing the body asserted that one could be "rebalanced by bloodletting, blistering, purging by vomiting or anal purgatives, or other potions that would cleanse the body."

What is Self-Harm?

"[A] deliberate and often repetitive destruction or alteration of one's own body tissue, without suicidal intent . . . [Also described as] self-injury, self-mutilation, self-inflicted violence, auto-aggression, and para-suicide." Centre For Suicide Prevention (http://www.suicideinfo.ca/csp/go.aspx)
Nadine Jodoin, "A closer look at self-harm." *SIEC Alert*, January 2001, No. 43.

Who Cuts?

It's hard to say, because people are very secretive about this. At least one percent of the population cuts. In the teen population, the figure could be as much as ten percent.

Cutters:
- Are more often female
- Are usually from middle- to upper-class backgrounds
- Have average to high intelligence
- Are well-educated
- Have low self-esteem
- Often suffer from anger, or depression, or other personality disorders
- Have a high incidence of substance abuse

A third of all cutters expect to be dead within five years.

Why Cut?

People cut for a multitude of reasons, usually arising from childhood experiences:

- Sexual, physical, and emotional abuse
- Neglect (physical and emotional)
- Violence at home
- Loss of parent (death or divorce)
- Parental illness and substance abuse
- Hypercritical upbringing
- High expectations
- Chronic childhood illness or disability
- Dislike of body shape
- Inability to express emotional needs or experiences
- Inability to tolerate intense feelings
- Bullying and rejection by peers
- Racial harassment and oppression
- Fear and shame about sexuality

Myths

Cutters are psychopathic

Cutters are dangerous to other people

Types of Self-injurious Behavior:

Conterio and Favazza reported the following findings as a result of their 1986 survey[1]:

- Cutting: 72 percent
- Burning: 35 percent
- Self-hitting: 30 percent
- Interference with wound healing: 22 percent
- Hair pulling: 10 percent
- Bone breaking: 8 percent
- Multiple methods: 78 percent (included in above)

Help

If you self-injure, or you know someone who does, the following websites are helpful:

- S.A.F.E. in Canada: http://www.safeincanada.org
- S.A.F.E. Alternatives: http://www.selfinjury.com
- Self Injury: A Struggle: http://www.self-injury.net/links/information.php
- Self Injury: You are not the only one*: http://www.palace.net/~llama/psych/injury.html

*NOTE: this site provides a link to an IRC channel for those who self-injure and would like support

---

[1] http://web.archive.org/web/20030106003206/www.i-p-d.com/safehaven/libcut.htm#Demographics

JULIE BURTINSHAW is the highly acclaimed author of *The Freedom of Jenny, Adrift,* and *Dead Reckoning.* She is an editor at online magazine *Suite101.com* and has contributed to various periodicals and magazines, both on and offline. She is a member of the BC Federation of Writers and CWILL (Canadian Writers and Illustrators).